DEATH UNDER PALM TREES

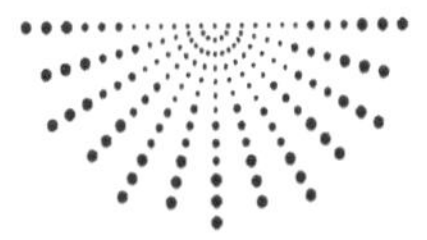

CARMEN RADTKE

Death Under Palm Trees

By Carmen Radtke

ISBN 978-1-9162410-6-0

- Jack Sullivan, war veteran and nightclub owner, on vacation
- Frances Palmer, his fiancée, a telephone exchange operator and occasional stage assistant to
- Uncle Sal, aka "Salvatore the Magnificent" Bernardo, ex-Vaudevillian and still the goods
- Katherine and Charles Parr, Jack's mother and stepfather
- The Right Honourable Mrs Walter Clifton (Aunt Mildred), reluctant hostess
- Tommy Clifton, her nephew, a rising talent in the diplomatic service
- Tinkerbell, Aunt Mildred's corgi

House guests and staff at "Les Palms"

- Dorothy Bassington-Whyte, Aunt Mildred's friend
- Walter Bassington-Whyte, her son, in the Foreign Office
- Lydia Bassington-Whyte, his sister
- Anne Deringham, a newly impoverished typist in the Home Office
- Peter Onslow, in the Home Office
- Dominic Jordan, in the Foreign Office
- Andrew Morris, in the Home Office
- Mr Bowman, a butler with more than one job
- Geraldine, a maid with an eye for a chance
- Bella Foster, Aunt Mildred's faithful lady's maid
- Sir Reginald Fitzpatrick, Tommy's superior, whose plans go wrong
- Colette Cobell, his niece and occasional spy in a good cause

CHAPTER ONE

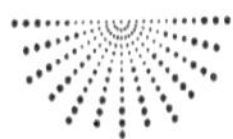

Frances Palmer hurried along Oxford Street, huddled into her woollen coat. Whatever people said about a mild December, for an Australian the dampness and wind in London cut straight to the bone.

She thrust her hands deep into her pockets. Until five minutes ago, they'd been toasty in knitted gloves. Now those garments, together with a scarf, kept a woman with a baby in her arms warm. Frances had encountered the pair trudging along towards the nearest soup kitchen, bare legs mottled with cold and the mother's face old with hopelessness. Yet she could have been no more than Frances's twenty-two years.

As exciting as London was with its bustling streets, grand buildings and magnificent shops like Selfridge's, her goal for this excursion, the poverty struck Frances much more than it did back home in Adelaide. Here in

England, nobody pretended to believe that 1932 would bring a return to prosperity. The stiff upper lip attitude smacked of habit, and of resignation.

Still, Frances had no reason to complain, with enough money in her pocket to replace scarf and gloves and still be able to buy a few presents for her family back home.

Outside the enormous building that was Selfridge's, Uncle Sal waved at her. He'd been to visit his old theatrical agent, dating from his heydays as "Salvatore the Magnificent", while Frances window-shopped. She'd enjoyed it more on her own than she had expected. Her fiancé, Jack Sullivan, had stayed behind with his mother.

Ever since they had arrived in London, answering an urgent if vague call for Jack's help, Frances had done her best to give them some space. She also refrained from prodding them for details about the purpose of their stay on the other side of the world. Whatever Jack's mother needed from him, his mum would decide when to tell him. For a fleeting moment, the thought crossed Frances's mind that Jack did know but couldn't tell her for some strange reason. She admonished herself. Jack had never lied to her. He would at least mention it to her if he couldn't divulge something.

Selfridge's, with its cream-coloured columns and stuccoed façade, took her breath away. She had first seen the store from the top deck of a bus, when Jack and Uncle Sal took her on a whirlwind tour of the city. Up close, she couldn't stop gawking at the Queen of Time clock, an eleven-foot bronze statue of a winged woman in front of two angled clock faces.

'Have you ever seen anything like it?' she asked Uncle Sal as she caught up with him. For Frances, this was her first proper voyage, but Uncle Sal had travelled half the world during his stage career as a vaudeville artist and was used to all sorts of marvels.

He smiled at her. 'She is really something special,' he said. 'And new as well.'

'New?' Her jaw came close to dropping. How could any store owner be that rich during this depression that had millions of people hungry and without a proper roof their heads?

As soon as they stepped inside the store, she could understand how. Dozens of shoppers strolled around, in the manner of people who were neither strapped for cash nor lacking leisure. Even the shop assistants possessed a refined air that Frances would never ever be able to imitate without huge effort. Three weeks in London had made her conscious about the stark differences that existed in Great Britain between the upper and the lower classes, and also between a native Londoner and a colonial girl like herself.

Uncle Sal gave her arm a light squeeze. He too went scarf-less, although he'd set out with a checked muffler wrapped around his neck. In his case, a one-legged veteran had been the recipient.

Frances inhaled the fragrant air, redolent of roses and

violets and orange blossoms. Her gaze kept wandering to the beauty counters. Enamelled powder compacts and swan's down powder puffs would make heavenly presents, and she could mail them without worrying too much about the postage or damages during the transport. She imagined her mother flicking open a compact and mentioning to her friends that Frances had sent it all the way from London.

'If you see something you fancy, love, go ahead.' Uncle Sal beamed at her. 'It's not as if we're here forever.'

'True,' she said. 'It can't hurt to ask for the price.'

Uncle Sal disappeared while a shop assistant helped Frances select the three prettiest powder puffs and compacts in the lower price range. She had expected the glamorous girl to look down on her, because the lady on the next counter didn't so much as mention money while she piled up a whole beauty arsenal, but instead the shop assistant suggested the best bargains without any prompting.

She wrapped Frances's purchases in elegant parcels as Uncle Sal joined her, with a large shopping bag in his hand.

'Tea, milady?' He offered her his arm.

'There's a Lyon's around the corner,' Frances said, proud of her newly acquired knowledge of local customs and popular places.

Uncle Sal winked at her. 'Good-oh. We'll save that for another day.'

Frances held her head high as they let the lift boy take them all the way up to the Palm Court restaurant. A waiter led them to a table directly underneath a glass roof, with large chandeliers glittering despite the dullness of the day. A few months ago, Frances would have gaped. Now, inured to opulence by their sea voyage on the *SS Empress of the Seas* and visits to the British Museum and the Old Vic theatre, she enjoyed her fancy surroundings without being overawed. Having Uncle Sal by her side also helped.

He didn't bat an eyelid at what must have been an enormous bill for their tea and an assortment of cakes. Everyone would have thought he was born to wealth, instead of growing up on the stage.

When she'd devoured the last morsel of Victoria sponge, Frances swept a crumb off the bottle green jumper Uncle Sal had given her for Christmas. The tweed skirt she'd bought herself, from a small dressmaker's shop Jack's mother frequented. They had one more treat in store before they took the underground back to Hampstead, where Frances and Uncle Sal occupied the guest bedrooms while Jack slept on a comfortable sofa in the study.

J ack already awaited them, in a crowd of expectant people. At his side stood his mother Katherine, wrapped in a camel hair coat with a fur collar, with a dark red hat on her silver-streaked brunette curls.

'Frances, darling. You'd better let Jack carry your parcels.' Katherine pecked her on both cheeks. 'I'm afraid it'll be an awful crush, but it can't be helped.'

As if on cue, the crowd moved forward. Jack and Uncle Sal shielded Frances and Katherine bodily, until they all came to a standstill to admire a small winged statue on top of the Shaftesbury Memorial Fountain. After a prolonged absence, Londoners were welcoming Eros back in its original pace in Piccadilly Circus. For nine years it had stood in the Embankment Gardens, while under their feet an underground station was being built.

Frances's heart drummed faster, but if she was honest, that had more to do with Jack's presence than the return of the statue, beautiful as it was.

'Shall we let others have our spot?' Katherine asked. 'There'll be plenty of occasions after your return to visit Piccadilly Circus, and at least you can say you were there on this special day.'

'Splendid idea. Shall we take a taxi?' Jack stepped out onto the street and beckoned a chauffeur.

During their ride Frances had to stop herself from pressing her nose against the window. Everywhere she looked there was something else to catch her attention. She wondered if Katherine ever got used to the wonders of London that not even the long lines of people outside the soup kitchens or the beggars with their handwritten signs could diminish. Or did she miss Australia, with its endless sunshine and a freedom for women that had allowed her to divorce Jack's irresponsible father? In England, she'd still have been married to him instead to Charles Parr, a man who adored her and had welcomed Jack, Frances and Uncle Sal with open arms.

She'd purchased a jar of honey for him. Tomorrow, Frances, Jack, and Uncle Sal were due to travel to the south of France, to spend a fortnight with friends they'd made on their voyage over.

A chuckle rose in her throat. If somebody had told her three months ago that Frances Palmer, a switchboard operator from Adelaide, would gallivant across Europe and be invited to perform as Uncle Sal's assistant, Signorina Francesca, she'd have called them barmy as a bandicoot. No, she silently corrected herself, here in the heart of the Empire, she'd have called them daft. But anyway, here she was, riding through London and bound to attend a New Year's party in Nice.

Aromatic logs crackled and blazed in Katherine's fireplace. The upper floor of an Edwardian terrace where the Parrs lived in what they called a maisonette, possessed a small morning room they also used for the meals, but in the afternoon, it no longer received any sunshine. The spacious living room with its large open fire, upholstered furniture, and a Christmas tree festooned with glass baubles, tinsel, and tinfoil birds, was by far the cheeriest place to have their afternoon tea, and it saved them from having to heat another room.

Until recently, Jack had supported his mother and stepfather financially, but when Charles had finally found employment again a year ago, they'd declared themselves independent.

He worked long hours, but today he had been able to join them for their tea and contentedly warmed his hands in front of the fire. His dark hair thinned at the top and wire-rimmed spectacles gave him a bookish appearance, but he possessed a dry wit that made him memorable despite his quietness. Frances had taken to him at once.

At one side of the room stood a baby grand piano, which Uncle Sal played in the evening. Frances had been surprised by both his delight and his talent. When they were back home, she'd see if they could afford an instrument of their own. Or he could play during closing hours at the Top Note, Adelaide's best nightclub which

Jack had opened in 1928. It enabled him to look after his family financially and to take care of a dozen or so men who'd served under Captain Jack Sullivan in the Great Stoush.

Childhood pictures of Jack and his sister, who now lived in New Zealand with her new husband, stood on the mantelpiece. On the wall hung a portrait of her. Jack had painted it as a Christmas present to his mother.

Katherine kept her gaze fixed on her daughter's likeness with a mixture of longing and pride as they drank their tea. Her husband put a sympathetic hand on her sleeve, and she gave him a brave smile that tugged at Frances's heartstrings. It must be hard to be separated by such a long distance, she thought, and to have a son-in-law she only knew from photographs, and through letters.

No wonder Jack had wanted his mother to meet Frances before they got married. She thought of her own mother, and how difficult it had been for her to have her son and his family living up in Queensland, more than a thousand miles away from Adelaide. Yet compared to the distance between England and New Zealand, they almost lived within cooee of each other.

Katherine had taken off her shoes and warmed her toes by the fire. A shawl around her shoulders protected her from any draught. She'd recently recovered from a cold, and Jack had reminded her to be careful. Her stillness and pensiveness struck Frances as unusual, so much had she grown accustomed to Katherine's quick wit and constant good humour.

'Is something wrong?' Jack said. 'If you want me to, I'll stay, and Frances and Uncle Sal can travel on their own to Nice.'

'Gosh, no.' Katherine smoothed her curls in a gesture much like her son's. She also had his blue eyes, but where his were deceptively sleepy, hers sparkled with a fire untouched by age. 'You go and have fun.'

'Are you sure?' Jack sat on the arm of her chair and wrapped his arm around her. She leant her head against his shoulder. 'You still haven't told me what you need my help with.'

'Absolutely sure,' Charles chimed in. 'Your mother's happiness is my responsibility, dear boy, and you've already done more than your share. You go and look after your bride and Uncle Sal.'

Frances shot them a sideways glance before she and Uncle Sal rose to give them some privacy. Katherine, whose cheeks had turned a becoming pink, motioned her to sit down again. 'I've lured you here under false pretences, I'm afraid.'

Uncle Sal and Frances exchanged a surprised look. Charles took off his spectacles to polish them, very much at ease, which in turn made Frances relax.

'I don't understand,' Jack said.

His mother stroked his arm. 'It's quite simple, darling. You've spent so many years taking care of all of us, which frankly saved us and a lot of others from ruin, but like Charles said, don't you think you should do a few things for yourself?'

She turned to Frances for support. 'The club is in capable hands, isn't it?'

'The best,' Frances said with conviction. Thanks to the wonders of airmail, they received weekly information about the well-being of both Top Note and their friends.

'And Charles and I are fine for money. All I wanted for you was to come here and take a few months for yourself, Jack. Do the things you really care about.' She gave the portrait, which had captured her daughter's face in exquisite detail, a pointed nod. 'Go, paint, be happy, let me organise a nice wedding, and when you return home with your wife, figure out a way to distribute the heavy load on your shoulders.'

Your wife. The words gave Frances a warm, fuzzy feeling in the pit of her stomach, but she also felt a pang of regret. It should have been her who saw what Jack was missing. Instead, she'd been so wrapped up in her happiness and her own responsibilities as breadwinner for herself, her mum and to a lesser extent, Uncle Sal, that she hadn't realised Jack made sacrifices too.

'Your mother's too right,' she said. 'This is a holiday. Make the most of it.'

Katherine twinkled at her son. 'Your sister put me up to it. I don't know where she gets that meddlesome streak from.'

'We'll see to it that things change a bit,' Uncle Sal said. 'I'm not out to pasture yet, and I do know my way around a stage, and the entertainment world.'

'See? All sorted.' Katherine sipped her tea. 'Shall we attempt to wangle tickets for a show tonight, or shall we have a quiet evening in?'

Jack kissed the hair on his mother's head. 'Let's stay home.'

'Excellent. I'll just arrange for our dinner.' Katherine rang a bell, to summon the elderly maid who also did the cooking and was the only servant the Parrs had. She went home in the evening, only to be back in order to serve them morning tea at eight. Frances's upbringing had at first demanded that she make her own tea, but she had caved to silent reproaches from the maid. In truth, she hadn't put up much reluctance. She enjoyed being spoilt for a while.

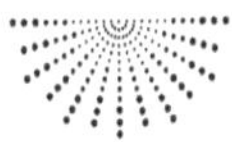

CHAPTER TWO

At the railway station, her future mother-in-law hugged Frances so tight she could smell the scented powder on Katherine's face. 'Enjoy yourself, dear child,' she said. 'The Cote d'Azur is lovely even in winter.' She pressed a bundle of glossy magazines and travel brochures into Frances's hands. 'If you have the opportunity, do visit the casino in Monte Carlo.' She chuckled at Frances's astonished expression. 'I'm aware you don't gamble, but it's such a beautiful palais it would be a shame to miss it.'

'I'll try,' Frances said and pecked Katherine on the cheek. Jack's mother had the same undefinable gift he possessed, to make people feel at ease. 'I wish you would come along,' she said.

'Lovely of you, but you'll be back before you know it.'

Katherine embraced her son. 'Do have fun, my darling. On your first night, take Frances and Sal to the Promenade des Anglaises, to watch the sunset on the water. Too, too utterly marvellous.'

It sounded blissful, Frances agreed. Standing at Victoria Station, waiting for the train to Dover, London hadn't lost its allure, but seeing the travel poster for the Riviera with its golden, green, and blue hues, made her heart ache for it. It looked almost indecently exciting against the backdrop of coal-blackened walls and the long line of people in shabby clothes who queued for a bowl of stew and a hunk of bread. How fast the fortunes of the world had changed.

The train pulled into the station and blew its whistle. The funnels belched and blew out steam.

Jack pulled Frances aside, away from the soot that accompanied the train's arrival. A porter stood a yard behind them with their luggage.

The three of them had the second-class compartment to Dover to themselves. They rattled through a landscape that in summer must be lush and inviting. At the end of the year it appeared desolate, with a few herds of cattle and sheep half shrouded in mist and the bare trees raising warning fingers into the low sky.

They had a hamper with refreshments with them, so they wouldn't have to search for the dining car.

Uncle Sal eyed it. 'I don't know about you two, but I could do with a bite. Railway travel makes me peckish.'

Frances's stomach rumbled, as if to agree. 'Much better than to eat on the ferry,' she said. 'Your mum said the crossing is bound to be rough.' She'd been spared seasickness on their ocean voyage, but then the big liner was built to withstand rough seas. A P & O ferry only meant for the English Channel might be less well balanced.

When they finished their repast, only hard-boiled eggs and fruitcake were left. Frances hoped they would be able to refill their thermos with tea in Dover. While their hostess, the Right Honourable Mrs Walter Clifton, or Aunt Mildred to them, had paid for their travel arrangements in return for their performance at her New Year's party, Frances intended to spent money prudently.

She was in luck. In Dover, another traveller who was on her way to take up employment as a nanny, showed her where she could help herself to hot water for her thermos. Once they'd reached Calais and were on the train, meals were included.

Frances inhaled the tangy air outside the French station. It had a balmier quality than on the other side of the English Channel, and the Golden Arrow that had taken them from London to Dover, changed its name to Fleche d'Or for the journey to Paris. She pinched herself to make sure this wasn't a dream. She really had arrived in France.

All around them bustled dark-eyed men with berets, smoking cigarettes and yakking away at rapid-fire speed. Women carried baskets with shopping as they hurried along the street.

'Ready to board?' Jack slung his arm around her shoulder, and they entered the station building, where Uncle Sal guarded their belongings.

'I can't believe we're in France,' she said. 'I mean, you've been here before but ...' She clapped her hand over her mouth. Of course, Jack had been in France before, fighting in the blood-soaked trenches. 'I'm sorry,' she said.

'Don't be. It'll be good to see the country in peace time.'

'It's a painter's paradise,' Uncle Sal said. 'Almost as good as Italy.'

Jack and Frances both grinned. Although Uncle Sal had left his native country as a small boy, his loyalty had never wavered. The only country that could compete in his opinion was Australia, where he'd spent the last seventeen years after half a lifetime touring from country to country. He had left Europe with months to spare before the war broke out.

'Do you speak French?' Frances asked the men. Her foreign language skills consisted of a few words of Italian

Uncle Sal had taught her and she fervently hoped she'd not have to deal with French people on her own.

'Not fluently, although I can get by.' Uncle Sal helped her onto the stepping board. 'We'll take care of you, won't we, Jack?'

'Too right we will.'

They settled in their compartment, which they shared with two silent nuns who whiled away the hours studying the bible.

Jack held Frances's hand as she watched the unfamiliar landscape fly by with an unsettling speed. The train to Melbourne which Frances had travelled on twice before had nothing on the Fleche d'Or.

After her original unease about racing along the tracks, the rhythmic chugging of the wheels lulled her into a doze. She'd spent most of the night before lying awake in Katherine's guest room, fretting over possible mistakes she might make in polite society.

When she woke up, they were just pulling into the Gare du Nord. From here a taxi would take them to the Gare de Lyons. Frances allowed herself to be bundled into the car. She rubbed her eyes, intent to shake off her drowsiness. After all, they'd drive through Paris, the most romantic city in the world. Gleaming, high buildings and wide avenues made her gawk. 'It's bonzer,' she said, lost for a better expression.

'We could stop here for a few days on our way back,'

Jack said with a wistful note in his voice. 'What do you think, Uncle Sal?'

Her godfather rubbed his hands in glee. His dark eyes shone with enthusiasm. 'Absolutely. I'll take you around Montmartre, and the Left Bank. Then there's the opera, and we mustn't miss the Louvre. But first, two weeks at the Riviera.'

'Mr Sullivan? Here's a telegram for you.' A middle-aged wagon-lit conductor in a crisp tunic handed Jack a sealed envelope. His lilting voice held only a trace of an accent.

A chill ran through Frances. A second ago, she'd revelled in the beauty of the station with its ornate iron-work and palm trees on the concourse, and the glory of the fabled Blue Train itself. Now, she silently prayed that the telegram did not contain devastating news. For someone, anyone, to pay for an expensive telegram, the matter had to be urgent.

The metallic taste of blood crept into her mouth. She had bitten her lip without noticing it.

'Thank you.' Jack managed a grateful smile as he slipped the envelope into his pocket. The conductor led Frances to a second-class sleeping compartment with two berths and a nifty fold-away sink in a corner. Her suitcase went into a luggage rack above the upper berth.

'Yours is the top one, Miss Palmer,' he said.

'Thank you.' Jack and Uncle Sal shared the compartment next to hers. She splashed cold water over her wrists, to help her calm down before she knocked on their door.

Jack unfolded the telegram as she sat down next to Uncle Sal.

'It's from Aunt Mildred,' he said.

A wave of relief swept over Frances. At least her family was safe. Annoyance followed. 'Does she no longer want us to visit? Why not ring us before we set off?'

Uncle Sal shushed her.

Jack perused the message. His jaw set in a grim line. 'She still wants our company, but she's afraid circumstances have changed. Something has happened, something bad. She's asking for our help, and she mentions our adventure at sea.'

'Another murder? That's fast becoming a bad habit, my boy.'

Frances agreed with Uncle Sal. Dead bodies and the solving of murder cases had become all too familiar during the course of this year. During their ocean crossing, Aunt Mildred and her nephew Tommy had joined their investigation into the death of a passenger with relish. But she knew from experience how different it felt if the case struck too close to home.

'I don't think so,' Jack said. He rubbed his clean-shaven chin. 'Whatever it is, Tommy is going to meet us in Nice and inform us in greater detail.'

At dinner in the plush restaurant car, the leg of lamb with rosemary potatoes and peas turned to ash in Frances's mouth. She'd grown fond of Aunt Mildred and her nephew Tommy. What if they were in trouble? Both Frances and Uncle Sal had been looking forward to being the guest stars at an elegant affair. It might be silly to pine for attention, but she couldn't help it.

Jack ate with good appetite, as did Uncle Sal. She pulled herself together. An empty stomach didn't change anything.

They retired early. The morning would bring them to their destination.

Frances's roommate already lay in bed. The blanket covered her to the tip of her nose, and she snored gently.

The woman had cranked up the heating too. Frances longed to fling the window wide open. London's air was the least agreeable aspect of the city, with its millions of chimneys and factories. She missed the sweetness of the countryside or the ocean where a lungful of fresh air always restored her.

She changed into her night dress with as little noise as she could before she climbed the short ladder to her berth.

The bright light from the overhead lamp ended a too short night. She peered down onto her roommate, a smart young woman with brisk movements. Dark, marcelled hair was topped by a coronet cap that, together with the apron over her neat blue dress, classified her as maid.

Outside, the world was still dark.

'I'm sorry to wake you,' the maid said. 'My mistress likes her morning tea at the crack of dawn.'

'No worries.' Frances stifled a yawn. 'Is it far until Nice?'

'We're just outside Fréjus. It should be light enough soon to catch a glimpse. It's ever so pretty.' The maid smoothed her apron and popped out of the door.

True enough, when Frances sat down with her companions for a breakfast of tea and flaky pastries whose name she couldn't pronounce, the winter sun shone on pastel-coloured villas and a glittering sea.

As they departed the train at Nice station, Frances spotted her roommate following an elderly lady to a waiting limousine. A uniformed chauffeur hastened to bow as he opened the door for them.

Jack followed her gaze. 'I can't imagine Bluey like that,' he said, mentioning his old sergeant and second-in-command who doubled as a driver when needed. He and his wife had become good friends with Frances and Uncle Sal, and while she could imagine the stolid Bluey in many roles, acting servile wasn't one of them.

A bad imitation of a kookaburra call alerted them to Tommy's presence. He stood half-hidden behind a tall palm tree. Jack gave him a quick nod, but to Frances's surprise their friend strolled away.

CHAPTER THREE

They caught up with Tommy in a side street, where he'd parked a large, cream-coloured Chevrolet.

Tommy's face shone with the same pink freshness Frances remembered, but his jaw was tense. He shook their hands with palpable relief. 'I say, smashing to have you here. I only wish it were under happier circumstances.'

He opened the door for Frances. She climbed into the back seat. Jack and Uncle Sal followed a few moments later after they put the luggage in the trunk.

Tommy drove away from the town, towards the gentle hills rising in the background. After a mile, he turned onto a rutted path more fitting for a farm wagon. He stopped the car behind a stone barn. 'Sorry if this is all frightfully hush-hush. I couldn't afford for anyone to overhear us.'

'Do you mind if we talk outside?' Jack said. 'We were cooped up all day yesterday.'

'Gosh, yes, by all means. If you'd like to take the rug to wrap around your knees, Frances, there's a spot to sit a few yards away.'

They settled down on a rustic bench under a cypress. Only Jack preferred to stand and stretch his legs.

Frances shaded her eyes against the sun blinking from an azure sky.

'It all began the day after we came home,' Tommy said. 'Aunt Mildred might not have mentioned that my late uncle used to be pretty well regarded in the Home Office and the Foreign Office too. She used to play hostess to more dignitaries than I've had hot meals.' He loosened his necktie. 'She'd planned a big soiree in London originally, with you as the guests of honour. Instead, my superior, who's kind of a big shot, asked her to come down here and arrange for a small house party.'

'Why here?' Jack asked.

'It's where she and my uncle used to come most winters, and they always invited a few guests. I was supposed to keep an eye out for anything unusual.' Tommy pulled a face. 'As you will have guessed, it didn't work too well. Yesterday, one of the house guests discovered that a few confidential papers were missing from his desk. He'd kept them locked away and only took them out when he was working.'

'Why would anyone take confidential papers along to a house party?' Frances asked.

'And why would anyone steal them, instead of taking photographs? Then, nobody would have been the wiser.' Jack rubbed his nose.

'We – that is, my superior, thinks they were taken, because they included blueprints.' Tommy glanced at Frances's blank face. 'Technical drawings. They were the originals, too. Stealing them increased the odds that nobody else had them or could replicate them.'

Jack broke into a slow grin. 'I'll bet you those papers were a trap. Why else go to the length of setting up this outfit?'

Tommy nodded his confirmation. 'Except that I have no idea who took the papers.'

'Would it have to be one of the guests?' Uncle Sal bent over to massage his gammy ankle. 'There must have been other people who knew of the papers, and the house, if Mildred came down here a lot.'

'That's our one piece of good luck.' Tommy sighed. 'I might have made an ass of myself because I couldn't spot a wrong 'un if he stood right under my eyes, but we have a small list of suspects. The house is a good three miles away from everyone else and the car was out of order with a flat tyre. The gate to the garden is always locked at ten, and so is the house. If it was an outside job, the man had help from the inside, because the papers disappeared between shortly before dinner and breakfast the next morning.'

'When do you dine?'

'At eight, and afterwards we play at cards or billiards, or go to town or drive up to Monte Carlo for a mild gamble. The night in question, we stayed in.'

'What do you expect us to do?' Frances closed her eyes and tilted her face to the warming sun. Outwitting a burglar sounded like fun. She much preferred to be able to show off their detection skills without a dead body involved.

It cheered her that Aunt Mildred thought highly enough of them to put her faith in their success. Stolen blueprints must be frightfully important, too.

'If you don't mind, we'd like Uncle Sal to be a bit mysterious and dodgy. Signor Bernardo, Italian gentleman of leisure and an old acquaintance of my uncle's. Frances could be his secretary. It's a rum do though.' Tommy gave her an apologetic look.

'No.' She shook her head. 'If there's a chance the thief still has the papers –'

'Nobody left the premises on his own, except for me, when I came to pick you up. And no other car came close. There's only one road leading to the house, and you can hear a motor from a mile away.'

'Are the police involved?' Jack asked.

'Heavens, no. The scandal would be terrible. My

superior has come down to Nice, that's all. He's waiting in his hotel for news from me.'

'Does he know about us?'

Tommy stared at Jack, aghast. 'Of course. Otherwise there'd be all kinds of trouble.'

'If the police aren't searching the rooms, you need someone else to do it.' Frances remembered last night's roommate. 'I could be the new maid. They do all the dusting and tidying, don't they?'

The pink of Tommy's cheek deepened. 'We can't ask that of you. I mean –' He faltered.

'It's our best shot,' Jack said. 'If you can arrange for a car, I'll be Signor Bernardo's chauffeur, if your aunt already has one.'

'Currently there's only a French cook we hired from an agency, Auntie's ladies' maid Foster who's been with her since her wedding day, a butler and two maids. One looks after the ladies, the other's the housemaid, an elderly Frenchwoman who comes with the house. I guess we could entice her to take a break and have Frances replace her.'

Tommy put a light emphasis on the word butler which caused Frances to wonder.

Uncle Sal had noticed it too. 'Is the butler your culprit, or does he work for you folks?'

'Am I that obvious?' Tommy's face fell.

'No.' Uncle Sal guffawed. 'We're that good. When do we start?'

'If you don't mind, right away.'

It would be no problem at all to fit Jack and Frances with a chauffeur's uniform and a maid's dress, Tommy said. He proposed to drive to Cannes, where they would not be spotted.

Frances had expected there to be problems with arranging matters, but either Tommy was a wiz, or his superior could work miracles, because a mere three hours after they'd stepped off the train, they were on the way to Aunt Mildred's, with the French maid already gone.

The house, as Tommy had called it, transpired to be a three-storeyed villa the shade of lemon sorbet. The shutters were painted a dazzling white, and a balcony wrapped around two sides.

The gravelled driveway up to the villa took up half a mile. The weather-beaten gardener, who lived in a small cottage by the heavy iron gate, rushed out of his abode to open it for them. Palm trees lined the drive, ending at a large garage which would have once been a coach house and stable.

At the side of the villa, French doors opened out to a wide set of marble stairs leading down to a lawn, with a fountain in its midst. The stairs were flanked by more palm trees. Their fronds would cast welcome shade in summer. Given their abundance, it didn't come as a surprise to Frances that the villa was known by *Les Palms*, a name that needed no translation.

The thick gravel crunched under their feet.

Aunt Mildred stood on the verandah. She cut an imposing figure with her dress of garnet silk that set off her silver hair, and her pince-nez on her nose.

'Finally,' she said to Tommy. 'You should have rung up to inform me of your tardiness.'

He hung his head. 'Sorry, Auntie. The domestic service agency took forever with the papers.'

Aunt Mildred harrumphed and peered at Frances, who struggled to keep a straight face. 'Let's have a proper look at you, girl.'

Frances curtsied. 'Yes, Madam.'

'You appear satisfactory,' Aunt Mildred declared, in a nice carrying voice. 'And the new chauffeur?'

Jack approached from the garage. In his hands he carried a small suitcase with his own stuff, and a carpet bag for Frances. They'd left most of their luggage in a hotel room in Cannes, where Uncle Sal waited to be picked up.

Aunt Mildred's gave him the once-over as well.

He doffed his chauffeur's cap. A quick smile flitted over Aunt Mildred's face. 'Follow me,' she said.

Frances and Jack trudged behind her, through the wide doors and into a marble hallway. At the side, a staircase with a wrought-iron banister ran up to the first floor.

A handsome, middle-aged butler in immaculate tails appeared out of a side room.

'Bowman, would you please show our new maid to her room and explain her duties? Sullivan, your accommodation is above the garage. Please pick me up in ten minutes.'

'Yes, madam.' Jack gave her a small bow that became deeper as Mr Bowman glared at him.

Faint noises came from the first floor. Aunt Mildred turned on her heels and flounced upstairs.

'Come with me,' Mr Bowman said as Frances picked up her carpet bag. She followed him to the end of the echoing hallway, where the kitchen and scullery were located at the left, and a servant's room and the butler's pantry were to the right. A small, wooden staircase led to small landings on the first and the second floor and then up to the attic with the servant's quarters.

Mr Bowman showed Frances to a small room with an iron bedstead, covered with a crimped bedspread, and a washstand with a mirror, a water jug and bowl.

He closed the door behind him and lowered his voice. 'If you need anything, my door is at the end of the landing, next to the bathroom. Or if you move the potted poinsettia on the window sill in the drawing room to the centre, I'll seek you out. It's Frances, isn't it?'

He didn't wait for an answer. Instead, he drew a sheet of paper from his pocket and handed it to her. 'We have only a few moments. You'll be expected for your midday meal in the servants' room in half an hour.'

He shimmered away, just like the inimitable Jeeves, Frances thought in recognition of her beloved P.G. Wodehouse novels. That esteemed author had given her a solid preparation for the dealings between the upper class and their personal servants. Luckily, all she had to do was tackle the housework. And to search rooms for clues leading to a clever thief.

She tidied her cap – really nothing more than a wisp of a head band – and studied the note Mr Bowman had given her. It contained the layout of the villa, and information about each room's occupant.

On the ground floor, the dining room, the drawing room, a library and a games room took up the rest of the space.

On the first floor was a large ball room, as well as Aunt Mildred and Tommy's suites.

The second floor held two bathrooms, one for the ladies and one for the gentlemen, and the guest bedrooms.

According to the note, the missing papers had been stolen from the bedroom of Peter Onslow, a university friend and Home Office colleague of Tommy's. The rooms adjoining his belonged to Andrew Morris from the Home Office and Dominic Jordan from the Foreign Office. The last of the gentlemen was Wilfred Bassington-Whyte from the Foreign Office. His mother Dorothy, an old friend of Aunt Mildred's, accompanied him. She had also brought her niece Lydia and Lydia's friend Anne Deringham, a secretary in the Home Office.

Frances's head whirled with all the names. She stashed the note in her slippers, for a closer perusal later. If anybody became suspicious about the sudden departure of one maid and the appearance of another and decided to search her room, this was the safest hiding spot she could imagine.

She went down, to ask where she should start her work. On the way, she tested the floorboards to see if they creaked or if they offered the thief an opportunity to sneak unnoticed into Onslow's room. The staircase, though worn from decades of servants running up and down, stayed noiseless until she reached the second to last step. It squeaked, audibly so. She took a step to the side and tested the edge. To her satisfaction, it stayed silent. Now she just needed to remember that.

Exactly ten minutes after Aunt Mildred had given him his orders, Jack opened the Chevrolet door to her. A yapping bundle of fur jumped out of her arms. Tinkerbell, Aunt Mildred's corgi, had recognised his old friend from his days at sea.

Jack picked him up and murmured into the twitching ear, 'I've missed you too.'

'Thank you, Sullivan,' Aunt Mildred said. 'Tinkerbell

appears to have taken a shine to you. He's an excellent judge of character.'

'He's a lively little fellow.' Jack closed the door behind Aunt Mildred and Tink and settled behind the steering wheel. He'd dropped his Australian accent. One new staff member from the edges of the Commonwealth was enough. Thanks to his early years in England, he could switch from one to the other without having to think about it.

On the way to Uncle Sal's hotel, they chatted about their respective Christmasses, and anything but the task ahead, saving Aunt Mildred the trouble to repeat herself.

The big car glided along the winding road with an ease that allowed Jack to admire the scenery. From the top of the driveway, he had enjoyed a glimpse of the sweeping Mediterranean Sea. Close by must be Cimiez, home of the painter Matisse. He wouldn't think of art now, Jack told himself. First, they had a mystery to solve.

A few props, and Uncle Sal's personality had changed. A white scarf around his neck, a cape lined with red silk around his shoulders and an ebony cane with a silver handle gave him an air of operatic sophistication.

The slender man in the room with him would have

paled in comparison if it weren't for the steely glitter in his eyes.

Jack took him to be in his late fifties, with the confidence of a man accustomed to wealth and importance.

'Reggie.' Aunt Mildred proffered both her hands. He planted air-kisses next to her cheeks. 'Meet my good friend, Jack Sullivan. Jack, this is Reginald Fitzpatrick, Tommy's superior.'

'My pleasure.' Fitzpatrick had a firm handshake, and his probing gaze reminded Jack of his old Colonel during the war.

'What exactly are we up against, sir?' Jack relaxed onto a chair and crossed his legs. If Fitzpatrick was to take them seriously, he had to accept them as equals. Showing deference would have sent the wrong signal.

'How much has Tommy Clifton told you?'

'Not much. Only that you suspected something was up with either the documents in question, or one of the guests assembled at *Les Palms*.'

Fitzpatrick inclined his head. 'That's correct.'

'What exactly is in those blueprints?' Jack paused. 'If you used them as a trap, or bait, I assume they aren't the real thing. Close enough to the original, probably, only slightly altered to make them unusable.'

Fitzpatrick gave Aunt Mildred a questioning glance.

'Nobody breathed a word, but it makes sense,' Jack said. 'I'm quite sure you checked my war records and other credentials. If we don't know what we're up against, you might as well save us the trouble of all this hush-hush stuff.'

'The blueprints are for a technical device used in aircraft radio transmission.' A muscle in Fitzpatrick's jaw twitched. 'Only there was a mix-up. Young Onslow, who was supposed to check the specifications, took the real ones instead of a set lovingly prepared by our experts in a backroom. Andrew Morris filed away the altered documents, but it seems someone forgot to tell him to remove the real ones, so the files sat side by side.'

'Onslow was in on it?' Uncle Sal stopped twirling his cane.

'Good lord, no. None of them were. We'd caught a few whispers, that there were other parties interested in that device, which is meant to significantly improve reach and stability of transmissions. So, we let slip that Onslow was behind on his schedule and would finish his work during a pleasure party.'

'How valuable is that invention?' Uncle Sal asked.

'In itself, we could live with it falling into the wrong hands. But it's imperative to find out who in our ranks is working against us.'

'You're sure that it's a proper leak? Men have been known to share office talk with their wives, or in their clubs,' Jack said.

'That's why we want your help. You can go where we

can't.' Fitzpatrick slammed his hand on the table. 'I'd hate to see lots of promising careers ruined over this.'

'There's something I don't understand. Why steal the documents now, when it's bound to cause a hullabaloo, at least behind closed doors. Why not wait until everyone's packing their bags? Ten to one, Onslow wouldn't have checked, or found a chance to raise the alarm.'

'Very astute. It was made clear to the household that Onslow had finished his work and was due to deliver himself of the documents within a day or two, in Nice.'

'Was made clear? Did Onslow tattle?'

Fitzpatrick snorted. 'Nothing so crude. A phone call that Mrs Clifton answered.'

'I simply used a tried and true method.' A satisfied gleam came into Aunt Mildred's eyes. 'I repeated the information in a clear voice while taking down a message. The door to the dining-room was open.'

'But Onslow's reaction might have given the game away.'

'The dear man was running an errand for Lady Bassington-White in town.'

'How risky is this affair? I won't have my little Frances walk into the lion's den and be left to fend for herself. Most crooks are all froth and no beer, but they don't go up against a whole government department,' Uncle Sal said. Jack nodded in agreement.

'Bowman, that's the man we planted as butler, is combat-trained. He'll guard her with his life.'

'Please, my dear?' Aunt Mildred touched Uncle Sal's hand. 'I understand it's not remotely what I promised you, but you three are our best hope.'

He gazed at Jack for his approval before he smiled at her. 'We've pulled other rabbits out of our hat, haven't we, Jack? We won't disappoint you, Mr Fitzpatrick. I'll act as shady as they come, and with any luck, your little rat will see if I have anything to offer in his line of work. I'm sure between you and Jack, you could come up with convincing drawings worth stealing.'

'Thank you. I won't keep you.' He handed Jack a slip of paper with a telephone number. 'You can leave a message here day and night.'

'There's a telephone box two miles down the road from the villa, and a bicycle at the back of the garage,' Aunt Mildred said. 'It might not be prudent for you to ring up from the house.'

~

Frances swallowed as she knocked on the open door of the servants' room. Her reading had taught her that a well-bred servant entered her lady's room without announcing herself. About how a maid behaved when joining other staff, the novels said nothing.

'Don't stand there dawdling,' a young woman not much older than Frances told her.

Frances slipped into the empty seat next to her. 'Thank you,' she said.

Mr Bowman presided over them at the head of the table. The cook, a sparrow-like woman with reddened hands and a pleasant smile for Frances, ladled an aromatic broth into soup plates and handed them around. Madame Petit, Frances remembered from the note. Cooks, married or not, were given the honorific title Mrs or Madame, just like the butler was Mr Bowman. Maids like Frances would be called by their first name, ladies' maids were called by the gentry by their last name, without an honorific title. So was the chauffeur. She had to remember that, just as she would have to remember not to use Tommy or Aunt Mildred when talking about her hosts.

'You'll find this a very pleasant house,' the motherly woman presiding over the other end of the table said. Her black dress and petticoat were made of fine wool, to an older fashion, yet the clothes looked as new. She must be Aunt Mildred's personal maid, Bella Foster.

'Is it many people we have to do for? Are the British gentry very demanding?' Frances sampled the soup. One spoonful, and she could have swooned. If all the meals were like this, she understood why the French were so proud of their cooking.

'It's only a small party,' the young maid said. 'I wouldn't know about you, but there've never been any complaints about my services.'

'That's enough, Geraldine,' Mr Bowman said. 'You

should consider yourself lucky that Frances has taken this position at such a short notice. Otherwise you might have had to pick up a broom.'

Frances glanced around under her lashes. Was anyone showing some doubt about her? No, she decided. Still, it would be good to see if the servants all were as harmless as they appeared. After all, if she could be smuggled into the staff as a spy, so could someone else.

'When did she leave?' she asked. 'Did you have to fill in for her as well?'

'Me?' Geraldine tossed her glossy curls. 'I have my hands full with my ladies, and with looking after the gentlemen's clothes, too.'

Foster clucked her tongue reproachfully. 'I'm sure we would all have done our bit to keep things ticking over. And it's nobody's fault the sister was taken ill and needed someone to mind her babies.'

'I reckon,' Geraldine said in a mollified tone. 'And madam was ever so generous. Putting her on the next train and paying for a sleeper and all. She gave her a tenner, too, to tide her over. And a few francs.'

'Gosh, that is nice,' Frances said. 'And this place is a beaut.'

Geraldine giggled. 'Doesn't she talk funny?'

'You're Australian, Mr Bowman told us. What brings you to France?' Foster gave her a kindly beam.

Frances swallowed another spoonful. She counted herself lucky she'd prepared for this kind of question with

Jack. 'My mistress took me with her when she moved back from Australia to London. But it's that cold and damp there in winter, her doctor said needed a warm climate.' Frances pulled a tragic face. 'I wish he'd recommended a place without a casino.'

'Monte Carlo? I've never been.' Geraldine's mouth formed a wide o. 'What happened?'

'She lost. Can't you see that in poor Frances's face? Now stop badgering the child,' Mrs Foster said.

'Wait a moment. If you were her lady's maid, don't you get any ideas in your head. You're here to do the cleaning.' That explained Geraldine's barbed remarks. She thought Frances was angling for her own position.

'Gosh, no. I mean, too right I wouldn't dream of barging in. I'm glad the agency put my feet under this table.' Frances laid her native accent on as thick as she could. Most English servants seemed to consider anyone speaking differently as a bit stupid. That way, they'd pay her less attention.

'Finish your soup, girls,' Mr Foster said. 'Cook has made sandwiches too, and we need to let her return to work.'

'Is there anything I need to take special care of, with the guests? When I do their rooms, I mean?' Frances gave them a wide-eyed, innocent look.

'That Lydia is a bit of a handful,' Geraldine said, much friendlier now she no longer saw Frances as a rival. 'The number of times I almost stepped into cigarette ash on the floor or spilt powder, and that with the wicked prices she pays for her cosmetics. Her friend is much more careful, and Lady Bassington-Whyte, now she is a real lady.'

'Only Mrs Clifton and Lady Bassington-Whyte have a fireplace in their bedrooms,' Mr Bowman said. 'You need to clean the grates and prepare a good fire ready to be lit. The ladies also take their morning-tea in bed. You fetch it from the kitchen, and Geraldine carries it into the bedrooms.'

Geraldine's face took on a faintly smug expression.

'After lunch, you can start with the gentlemen's rooms. They're usually occupying themselves in the games room until dinner.'

Frances nodded. 'Good-oh.'

Crumpled pyjamas and a dressing gown were strewn over Wilfred Bassington-Whyte's unmade bed. Frances bit her lip as she tried to figure out what to do with them, until she remembered Geraldine's claim to responsibility for clothes.

She felt under the mattress as she tucked in the rumpled sheet. Nothing. She made the bed, folded the clothes and put them on the duvet. A little light dusting and sweeping, and the room was as neat as possible.

The wardrobe held an array of suits, shirts and sweaters in addition to formal evening dress and shoes and nothing else. The desk and the dresser possessed a locked drawer she itched to have a geek into. Uncle Sal had taught her how to pick locks, but he had with him the set of skeleton keys she needed.

In a pinch, she might be able to explain away a plan of the house. Skeleton keys though pointed to burglars. Or stage tricks, like they were supposed to have performed tomorrow night. A tiny stab of regret shot through her. Then she pulled herself together.

She lifted the chair cushion and swept out a few crumbs. The only place she hadn't searched yet apart from the drawers, was the top of the tall wardrobe. She'd need to climb onto a chair for that. Maybe she could risk it tomorrow.

A car purred up the driveway. Frances peeked out of the window, to see the Chevrolet come to a halt outside the house. She chuckled. They were all back together.

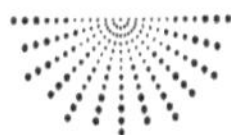

*U*ncle Sal dug his cane deep into the gravel and flung his scarf around his neck. Jack carried the luggage, two brand-new monogrammed leather suitcases that replaced Uncle Sal's treasured old trunk which was covered with labels from places that held fond memories.

With only a few hours to work with, or at most a day after Aunt Mildred suggested roping them in, Fitzpatrick had done a splendid job, Jack thought. If Bowman was half as efficient, they should be able to pull this investigation off. Unless the cove in question had long since fled the coop, but from what they knew, it was unlikely.

Bowman opened the door and bowed to Uncle Sal and Aunt Mildred. 'Sir. Madam.'

Jack stayed a few feet behind them as he followed

them up to the first floor. Uncle Sal was to occupy an empty suite that shared a bathroom with Tommy's. It was also the one nearest to the servants' staircase, making it easier for them all to meet in secrecy.

Jack wished he could stay in the house as well, although sleeping over the garage had the advantage that he could sneak away on the bicycle. He'd also hear if anyone helped themselves to the car. The gardener would not be in their way. He had been given a week's leave starting tonight.

Jack sauntered down the wooden staircase, only to have to squeeze to the side to let a smart young maid pass. She stopped and mustered him over the laundry basket she carried. Dimples showed in her cheeks as she twinkled at him. 'Thank you ever so kindly. You must be the new chauffeur.'

'My pleasure,' Jack said.

'Geraldine,' Bowman called from downstairs. 'Your work doesn't do itself.'

She rolled her eyes at Jack. 'I'll see you at dinner.'

Jack rubbed his neck as he followed at a safe distance. The last thing they needed was a flirtatious maid. Meeting Frances and the others would be difficult enough for him, without Geraldine lying in wait. Any interest she might develop in him needed to be nipped in the bud.

'Ready?' Aunt Mildred picked a piece of white fluff from Uncle Sal's velvet collar. The shoulders had been padded discreetly, just like all the garments had been tucked in to make them appear tailor-made for his trim figure. His own clothes, including his tuxedo and his dinner jacket, were fine for Uncle Sal or Salvatore the Magnificent. For Signor Bernardo, he of the as yet unspecified important connections and deep pockets, only the best would do, to fool the guests at *Les Palms*.

Uncle Sal offered her his arm. Together, they swept down the staircase. Every few steps, Uncle Sal limped. Instead of hiding the gammy ankle which had ended his professional career after a road accident, they'd decided to use it to its fullest. An honoured guest, who had trouble walking too much, could be forgiven if he asked for the attention of a valet, or in his case, the chauffeur's services.

The ladies whiled away the afternoon in the library. A petite blonde with a heart-shaped face and shrewd eyes sat engrossed in a French copy of *Vogue*. Next to her, a trim, dark-haired girl leafed through Agatha Christie's *Mystery of the Blue Train*. Uncle Sal thought that she skimmed the pages, if she read them at all.

A lady with a strong resemblance to the blonde girl stitched away at a tapestry. That meant the dark girl had to be Anne, the secretary, and the blonde had to be Lydia.

They glanced up as Mildred closed the library door behind them.

'May I ask you to welcome Signor Bernardo? He used to be a friend of my dear husband's.'

'How delightful.' Lady Bassington-Whyte put her tapestry aside and allowed Uncle Sal to kiss her hand. She wore a large square-cut diamond on her hand, and her tea-dress was cut in the latest fashion. The two young women were equally chic, as befitting the Riviera.

Muffled voices announced the arrival of the gentlemen, led by Tommy. 'Here's the rest of our merry party,' Mildred said as she introduced them.

Uncle Sal seized them up, one by one. Young Bassington-Whyte, who had a thatch of straw-coloured hair smoothed back with brilliantine, stood slouched by the door. He only straightened up to shake Uncle Sal's hand. His eyelids drooped. Either he played the part of the bored young man of leisure, or he operated on too little sleep and too much booze, although Uncle Sal doubted that. For lively young people, this house offered little in the way of entertainment, due to its remote location.

Dark-haired Onslow gripped his hand in a firm shake. The skin on his thumbs and index fingers was roughened. Uncle Sal guessed that he liked to work with his hands in his spare time. If he'd been responsible for confirming technical specifications, he likely possessed training as an engineer. His flannels were serviceable but not new, and his thin, mobile face betrayed nothing but friendly interest. If the theft had affected him at all, he hid it well.

Morris's face showed well-bred blankness. Of all the

guests, he was the least memorable, with his average build, average height, and brown hair. Uncle Sal wondered if he intentionally made himself disappear into the background.

Jordan shook Uncle Sal's hand with enthusiasm. 'Smashing of you to liven up your days. D' you play billiards, or whist?' His thin moustache and wavy dark hair could have belonged to a matinee idol, and his flannels were just the right side of comfortable, yet stylish for this kind of gathering, Uncle Sal thought approvingly.

'Looking for a new victim, Jordan?' Bassington-Whyte smirked. 'Tired of beating us?'

'It can hardly be called good sport, with the sad amount of challenge the two of you have to offer me.'

'I must confess I'm not much of a card man, unless if you would count the poker.' Uncle Sal had chosen the resonant yet velvety voice he'd spent years on perfecting. A light sprinkle of grammatical errors would be enough to make sure they all regarded him as a foreigner and as such, not to be taken quite as seriously as if he were one of them.

'The poker? Ah, you mean the game.' Jordan's lips twitched.

Uncle Sal gave him a haughty glare. 'That is what I said. The poker.'

Aunt Mildred broke into a silvery laugh. 'In that case you will be delighted to hear that the car is fixed and I have hired a chauffeur to see to it that you can go out and enjoy yourselves without having to worry about anything.'

She fixed her pince-nez on Tommy, who broke into a mild protest. 'I say, Auntie, that flat tyre wasn't my fault. If they'd tar or shingle that road properly, one wouldn't swerve and hit a rock. Besides, I put on the spare myself.'

She patted his arm. 'I know, dear. Would you be a pet and show Signor Bernardo around? I'm sure he'd enjoy a turn in the gardens before our afternoon tea.'

Tommy gave the other men a comical eye-roll. Anne was watching them from behind her novel, although it was impossible to tell what kind her interest was.

Uncle Sal inclined his head. 'Most gracious of you.'

The bright sun warmed Uncle Sal's face. In London, it had been a sickly circle in a leaden sky. Here, it cast golden streaks over the marble staircase at the back of the house. It dappled the palm fronds and made the roses and mimosas glow in a way that rivalled their Australian cousins.

Their fragrance scented the soft air. He inhaled deeply. 'Bellissimo.'

He was far from fluent after decades of living abroad, but a sprinkling of Italian here and there would go a long way in establishing his character.

'Careful, Mr Bernardo.' Tommy steadied his elbow as

they descended. The pink-veined marble had its drawbacks, despite its beauty. Anyone with good sense would have chosen a material that offered more grip, especially after a good shower.

'I'm glad to see your aunt so well,' Uncle Sal said. 'This place must be a tonic for her. Much better than the miserable weather on your small island.'

'You can't fault the Riviera,' Tommy agreed. 'My aunt was delighted you could join us. I hope you don't have to leave too soon. But you're retired, aren't you?'

Uncle Sal hesitated with his answer. He'd heard a window open in the villa, and a faint trail of cigarette smoke wafted towards them. 'The retirement, it is an ugly word,' he said. 'Let us say, I am fortunate to be a man of many interests, so life, it does not become boring.'

'Jolly good,' Tommy said. They strolled towards a tennis court. The markings were fading, but it seemed to be in good shape and well-used, which Uncle Sal remarked upon. On one side, a stand of pine trees flanked the court.

'We also play the occasional garden croquet, and there's an orangerie at the end of the lawn that gives you a magnificent view of the sea. We use it for picnics when the weather's fine enough for the ladies.' Tommy gave him a confidential shrug. 'Not much else to do here, I'm afraid. Although with the car back in business, we can always go out for a bit of fun in town.'

They fell silent as they strolled half a mile towards the

orangerie, a domed, octagonal room with the upper half made completely out of glass and iron. Inside, lush green plants, a fountain and enough seating for a dozen people made this the perfect place for afternoon tea. Or for a clandestine meeting.

Uncle Sal took a gander around. A lizard climbed up the fountain, and outside, birds searched for worms in the grass. They were bound to fly off if another human came close.

'Have you searched this place?' he asked.

Tommy's eyebrows shot up. 'You think the papers might be hidden here?'

'If there's a way to come here without being seen, it's safer than keeping the documents in the house.' Uncle Sal slid his cane under the loose cushions on the chaise and the chairs and tapped the floor for loose tiles. To a naturalised Australian it went against the grain to use his hands to poke anywhere critters might hide.

Tommy had no such qualms. He lifted potted plants and climbed onto the table to feel inside the lampshade. 'Nothing,' he said with a note of regret. 'Unless we're too late.'

'How close are we to the road?'

'About half a mile, I'd say. A chap could drive up and park the car in one of the driveways of an empty villa. There's a couple of places that are empty for the season.' Tommy's eyes sparkled as he warmed to his theme. 'It's a bit of a trek, and you'd have to climb over a high fence, but, by golly, it should be doable. I think we're onto something here.'

'Good. Or rather, molto bene. Is there anything else to see?'

Tommy shook his head. 'Only the shed where we keep rackets and stuff, and that's next to the garage and locked at night.'

Jack polished the Chevrolet until it gleamed. He'd wondered why none of the guests had complained about only one vehicle for the lot of them, until he found the business card of a local taxi company in the toolbox. It made more sense to shell out for a hired car when the Chevrolet offered too few seats than to keep an additional motor.

'Coo-ee.'

He put down his polishing cloth as he heard Frances. 'Yes, miss?' he asked as he wiped his hands on a rag before he faced her.

She lowered her gaze. 'Mr Bowman said for you to come to dinner in an hour, and you're wanted to drive the ladies and gentlemen later.'

'I'll be there.'

She flashed him a grin before she darted off.

He chuckled to himself. Frances seemed to enjoy her role, and Uncle Sal was bound to love every second. He'd rubbed off on her. As for Jack, he didn't mind, as long as they reached their goal. And maybe Uncle Sal had rubbed off on him too. Shedding the skin of Jack Sullivan, successful businessman and at ease in any company, and becoming Jack the chauffeur and valet, was definitely a new experience.

He picked up the cloth.

Yet another knock interrupted him. 'I say, do you mind?' a wiry young man asked as he stepped inside with his stockier friend. From Fitzgerald's description, this had to be Onslow.

'Not at all.' Jack decided on a posture that showed respect without being subservient. 'What can I do for you?'

Onslow's gaze latched onto the Chevrolet, while his companion glanced around the room, including the work bank and the board for the keys. 'My friend Morris doesn't believe me when I tell him this is a stove bolt six.'

Jack grinned at the expression which had been coined in America for this particular motor. 'You have an interest in automobile engines?' Jack opened the sleek bonnet.

Morris and Onslow peered inside. 'I like cars,' Morris said. 'This is a pretty runner.'

'I wouldn't call her a runner,' Onslow said. 'Not with only 46 horse power.'

'She's fast enough for her purpose.' Jack closed the bonnet. 'Not everyone can afford a Daimler Double-Six.'

'Sadly.' Onslow pulled a face. 'I wouldn't mind one of those.'

'You'd only take the engine apart to see if you can increase the speed, which is already more than you could handle.' Morris pulled him away. 'Thanks for showing us…'

'Sullivan,' Jack said.

He gazed after them, intrigued. Had they really come because of an interest in engines, or did one of them want to discover where Jack kept the car key?

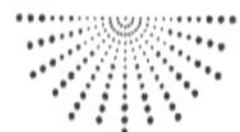

CHAPTER FIVE

Frances paused in the passage outside the guest bedrooms, trying to remember everything she had learned while tidying the rooms. Mr Onslow, Mr Morris, Mr Jordan and Miss Anne were all little work. The first two had even attempted to make their own beds.

'Hello?' A handsome young man ambled towards her. She had been so lost in thought, she hadn't heard him. 'You must be the new maid.' His teeth shone very white underneath his small, dark moustache as he gave her an appreciative smile. He remaindered her a little of matinee star John Gilbert, although this man had less regular features.

'Yes, sir.' She curtsied.

'Would you be so kind to bring up more towels?' He

pressed a coin into her hand. She felt heat rise in her cheeks. 'Of course. I'm so sorry.'

'Don't be. It's not your fault. I just prefer to have a couple of bath sheets ready in my room for my ablutions.' Without another word, he opened a door and stepped through it. So, that was Mr Jordan she thought. He'd given her a guinea. A nice, generous man, then.

U ncle Sal used all his bonhomie to establish himself at dinner as a man worthy of Aunt Mildred's friendship. He listened with rapt attention and a ready smile to Lady Bassington-Whyte's rambling reminisces about the delightful parties they all used to have in this very house, when a full staff of maids and valets and footmen had been employed. When she broke off with a flustered glance at Aunt Mildred, he complimented her on her dress, and the stiff upper lip which was the envy of other nations.

At the other end of the table, Lydia giggled at Onslow and Jordan's remarks. Bassington-Whyte showed signs of animation whenever he spoke to Anne and glared at Morris on those rare occasions when that young man spoke to her. The young lady divided her attention equally between her friend and the young men.

Aunt Mildred gave them all a fond look. 'I've arranged for tickets to the Palais de la Jetée, Signor

Bernardo. An operetta and afterwards a light supper and dancing should make a nice change.'

'How much time do I have to change?' Lydia's face lit up as she pushed back her chair.

'There's no need to hurry, child.' Aunt Mildred signalled the butler. 'We'll have our coffee in the drawing room, Bowman.'

'If you care for a snifter and a cigar, Mr Bernardo, we'd be happy to have your company in the library,' Tommy said.

Frances envied Mr Bowman whose position enabled him to enter most rooms without raising any question. She on the other hand, found herself stuck in the kitchen, doing the dishes together with Madame Petit. If only she spoke French, or the cook had more than just a rudimentary knowledge of English, she might have enjoyed a fruitful chinwag. Instead, she stood at the large stone sink, drying copious amounts of delicate china. Where the staff ate from earthenware, the ladies and gentlemen dined off gilded porcelain.

The cook had scraped the leftovers into two bins. One was for the cochon, she said. Seeing Frances's blank stare, she gave a spirited oink.

Frances hazarded a guess. 'A pig?'

Madame Petit rewarded her with a wide grin that

revealed two missing teeth. Her sunny expression vanished as she picked up the dessert plates. Two of them held a golden pudding with only one forkful taken.

Frances's mouth watered from the vanilla aroma. No wonder Lydia maintained that fashionable boyish slimness. The second plate belonged to Mr Jordan, but many men were less fond of sweets than women.

What a shame to see those puddings thrown away. Frances had no idea if the cook would understand her, as she said so, but her downturned mouth as she pointed at the dessert needed no translation. The cook patted her on the shoulder and gave her a nod.

'These English, they have no …' The words failed her.

'Well, I'm Australian, and I think your cooking is bonzer.' Frances kissed her fingertips to illustrate her words, a gesture borrowed from Uncle Sal.

The cook giggled. Frances relaxed. Maybe there was a way to communicate after all.

A bell jingled twice. Frances gazed around, until she spotted a bell board next to the door jamb. A lightbulb glowed red. Labels told them which room the bells connected with.

The rings were for the drawing room. Cook filled a silver pot from the coffee maker she seemed to have constantly on the go and put it on a tray. She signalled Frances to take it.

'I'll be back in a jiffy,' Frances said.

Outside the drawing room door, she attempted to

recollect what Jeeves would have done. Since she needed both hands to carry the tray, she either had to clamp down the handle with her elbow or put down the tray.

Geraldine saved her from her indecision. Although she snickered as she saw Frances's dilemma, she worked the handle for her.

Frances entered the room with less elegance than a real servant would have done. The ladies did not react. Only Aunt Mildred and Lady Bassington-Whyte shared the settee in front of the fire.

'I wish they would not encourage all this drinking and gambling so much at the Riviera.' Lady Bassington tugged on her lace-edged handkerchief. 'Don't you worry about Tommy?'

'He's a sensible boy, and I'm sure your Wilfred is the same.'

'Of course.' Lady Bassington-Whyte gave a forced little laugh as she noticed Frances. 'Black coffee for me, please.'

Frances poured two cups and waited for further instructions. Aunt Mildred took her after dinner coffee with a lump of sugar, but a new maid would be unaware of that.

'That's all,' Aunt Mildred said as she helped herself to sugar.

'Yes, madam.' Frances curtsied.

In the hallway, she allowed herself a small moment of triumph before she returned to her duties in the kitchen. If

Lady Bassington-Whyte disapproved of frivolous entertainment, she would have shunned a place like Nice. Which meant that she had reason to worry about Wilfred, either because he drank too much, or he lost more money than he could afford. Which might be a good motive to steal valuable documents.

If only she could share this insight with Jack and Uncle Sal. But they'd be off soon, to have fun on the town, while she spent her evening working or asleep in her attic room.

'Welcome to our little flock,' Mrs Foster said as soon as the butler had introduced Jack as the new chauffeur and occasional valet.

Geraldine simpered at Jack until she caught the butler's disapproving glance. Frances kept her eyes lowered, as befitted a junior servant.

'Thank you.' Jack accepted a helping of stew and smiled at the round. 'I'm glad to be here.' He ate faster than normal, so he could freshen up before taking his passengers on their evening jaunt.

'What a pleasant young man,' Mrs Foster said as he'd dashed off. 'Although I don't mind saying I was surprised that the mistress decided on hiring a driver after all.' She broke off. 'But that's none of our business, I'm sure.'

Mr Bowman ate the last bite on his plate before he

gave them the same explanation Aunt Mildred had prepared for her guests. 'This must not leave the room, but madam has been asked by certain well-placed gentlemen to show Mr Bernardo the kind of treatment he's accustomed to. Which is why she employed Sullivan.' He gave a gentle cough.

'The Italian gentleman? What makes him so special then?' Geraldine wondered.

'Nothing that should concern us,' Mrs Foster said. 'Or that we should gossip about. It'll all be as it was when the master was still with us.'

'Those were lovely times.' The maid's face took on a dreamy look. 'All those parties, and us travelling to foreign places like Paris and the Highlands.'

Mrs Foster pursed her lips. 'I remember you complaining about the perishing cold in Scotland and having chilblain.'

'It can be lovely and cold.' Geraldine beamed at Frances. 'And anyway, it wouldn't be me doing the worst chores, now would it? Scrubbing those flagstones and stuff.'

'You come off lightly enough, my girl. Don't think it'll always be all rosy, with us keeping the house running while madam is gone for months.' Mrs Foster addressed Frances. 'The mistress and Mister Tommy just recently returned from visiting your native country.'

'Australia? Good-oh. That is, I hope they liked it. And you all stayed behind?'

'Mr Bowman isn't on the day staff. He works for an important agency in London that sends them to work for foreign maharajas and film stars when they come to England. But when our mistress needs Mr Bowman, they wouldn't dream of saying no.' Geraldine clutched her chest, lost in visions of her own.

'It was much more convenient to travel unencumbered, and madam is used to lowering her standards when it's necessary.' Mr Bowman flicked an invisible crumb off his lapel.

Frances inwardly bristled at the butler's condescending tone, but she kept her serene expression. 'It cost my former mistress a fortune to come back home, even with me in a four-bed cabin.'

Geraldine sniffed. 'This household doesn't stint on anything. Why, we even received our full pay while madam was away.'

'Gosh,' Frances said. 'But then everyone in this house seems to be rich.'

'Hah. I could tell you things …'

'Geraldine, you'd better watch your tongue,' Mrs Foster said. 'We do not want idle gossip.'

'It's not gossiping if it's only us, right, Mr Bowman?' The maid's lip wobbled. 'All I'm saying is, when you find IOUs in coat pockets, and cheap shifts I'd be ashamed to wear underneath all that silk and satin, it makes you wonder.'

'IOUs? Aren't those notes that rich people write when

they owe money?' Frances widened her eyes in fake innocence.

'It's not Mister Tommy, I hope.' Mr Foster appeared shocked.

'No, it's –' She stopped, with a mulish expression on her face.

'Well?' Mr Bowman prompted her. The maid pressed her lips together, still saying nothing.

Mr Bowman gave in and changed tack. 'Anything that does not affect madam or sir is none of our business. You'd do well to remember that.' He gave both Geraldine and Frances a pointed look which Frances took as a reminder to keep her eyes peeled for these IOUs.

Geraldine changed colour. 'Yes, Mr Bowman.'

'And you should also keep in mind that madam does not approve of dalliances among the staff,' Mr Foster said. 'As personable as our new chauffeur is, I would recommend you remember that. That goes for both of you girls.'

Now Frances felt unwanted heat rise in her cheeks as she nodded.

'Good.' Foster patted Geraldine's hand. 'I'm sure you'll meet another nice young man, who can afford to support a family.'

Frances shot the butler a quick glance. Was it possible that Geraldine deserved a spot on their list of suspects? If she had been forced to give up a boyfriend she was sweet on, because he didn't have a bean, she might be a perfect target. She had easy access to all the rooms, and she knew the layout of the property as well.

To her surprise, instead of cook, the maid helped Frances with the dishes.

'Don't get used to me being here,' Geraldine said as she filled the deep stone sink with hot soapy water. 'Cook is allowed to go and see her daughter twice a week. She'll be back early enough to prepare breakfast though.' She rinsed the first plate and put it in a drying rack where Frances picked it up.

'Do we need to let her in?' If cook had her own key to the back door, she might have given it to an accomplice for copying. If Mr Bowman's superiors hadn't already talked to the local locksmiths, they needed to do that.

'Afraid you have to get up early? You'll be up before six anyway, to light the fires and heat the boiler. On cook's nights off, Mr Bowman leaves the back door on the latch and she takes her key.'

'Do the guests complain about noise? I mean, she probably has to go up to her room in the attic.'

'They don't hear a thing, although you'd better tiptoe downstairs in the morning, just in case.' The maid motioned at Frances's shoes. Despite their modest heels, they did clatter on the stone floor, unlike cook's rubber soles.

'What do we do if someone asks for coffee or a bite when she's away?'

'You'll make it.' Geraldine giggled. 'Honestly,

Frances, you should see your face. It's fine. They don't know about the arrangement and why should they? But even if they did, the ladies eat hardly anything, to stay thin, and the gentlemen are much more interested in their nightcaps.'

'Is there much boozing going on?'

'Mrs Clifton wouldn't stand for it if she had any idea, but the other maid told me she took empty bottles out of Mr Jordan and Mr Bassington-Whyte's rooms more than once.'

'Must be nice to be rich.'

Geraldine clanged the cutlery as she washed it. 'Lucky for some. Although I'd like to know why Mr Bassington-Whyte doesn't pay off his gambling debts. Or why Miss Anne has darns in her clothes. You wouldn't think it to look at her, but her shoes are all resoled.'

She lowered the pots into the sink. 'That new chauffeur is a dish, don't you think?'

'Are you still not finished?'

Frances gave a start as Mr Bowman spoke. He'd entered the kitchen without her hearing his steps.

Geraldine was equally surprised. 'Sorry,' she said.

'I hope you won't make Sullivan's position difficult.' The butler gave them a stern frown. 'He needs this employment to support his widowed mother and two sisters, he told me. As for madam, it would be a blow to her to have to let him go, if there's any sign of improper behaviour.' His face took on a sombre mien. 'Sullivan used to serve in her late nephew's battalion, and the opportunity to talk about him is a rare comfort to her.'

Frances admired the ingenuity Mr Bowman demonstrated. A bond like that would allow Aunt Mildred to go for solitary rides or a chat with Jack, and nobody would dare say anything.

'That awful war.' Geraldine gave the last pot a vicious rubbing. 'It's hard to think about it in a pretty place like this.' For an instant, they all fell silent, until the butler left as noiselessly as he'd entered.

'As if I needed a lecture on how to behave,' Geraldine said, but without the sting Frances had expected. 'What's wrong with looking at a nice man anyway? It's not as if I'd do anything, with me being as good as engaged.'

She basked in Frances's open admiration. 'My Bill's ever so handsome too. Foster says he's a ne'er-do-well, but she's wrong. As if it's his fault the bakery had to let him go.'

'He's a baker?'

'He'll open his own shop if we ever find the money.' Geraldine dried her hands on her apron and untied it. 'If you'll rub down the stove, we're all done.'

'Do we go to sleep now?'

'I'll wait up until the ladies are home. Didn't you help your former mistress undress?'

Frances should have thought of that. 'Only when there was a special occasion.'

'Well, this isn't Australia. We do things a bit different here, proper-like you might say.'

'I can see that,' Frances said in a humble manner, while she made a mental note to rearrange the poinsettia in the way Mr Bowman had mentioned. They needed a chinwag.

Uncle Sal had insisted on taking the taxi together with the young gentlemen, while Jack drove the ladies to their evening's entertainment.

He'd helped Aunt Mildred onto the passenger seat. 'Thank you, Jack,' she said with just enough warmth in her tone to emphasise their cover story, but not be overly familiar.

In the back, Lydia powdered her nose and Anne smoothed the fur stole she wore over her evening frock. Lady Bassington-Whyte twisted a handkerchief in her hands.

'Could you slow down, Jack?' Aunt Mildred asked. 'Lady Bassington-Whyte is afraid of speed.'

'Very well, madam.' Jack eased the foot on the throttle and saw the speedometer drop from 40 kilometres to 30. He did a quick mental calculation. That was less than 20 miles per hour. At this rate, the taxi would reach their destination at least ten minutes before they did. He hoped Uncle Sal would find a way to keep an eye of all his companions. It would only need a few moments for the thief to meet with somebody and arrange another date, or exchange information.

He accelerated a little as they reached the main road, with its smooth surface.

The winding road offered them a glimpse of the ocean, and palm trees. Villas nestled against the backdrop of the lush hills, and the lights of Nice competed with the sparkle of the stars above. Christmas had seen a full moon, and it still hadn't waned much.

It cast a glow on the inky water, and on the domed Palais de la Jetees that seemed to float on the sea like a fairy-tale palace.

He stopped the Chevrolet by the pier and opened the door for the ladies.

'You may park the car, and then come and wait for us in the café next to the gambling salon,' Aunt Mildred said.

'Very well, madam.'

Faint music greeted Jack as he walked with the stiff, measured gait of the professional servant across the pier. Gentle waves lapped its foundations, and ducks dozed by the rocky shore. The whole building appeared ablaze with light that shone out across the bay.

He wished Frances were here, beside him, and that he had his camera.

The Palais offered a multitude of rooms and entertainment, from restaurants which he ignored, to a ball room that Aunt Mildred would have to take care of, bars and gambling rooms.

The café offered him a good view of a bar where he spotted Uncle Sal and the young men. If only he could move freely, but a man in a chauffeur's uniform would stick out in most parts of the palais. He sat down with a coffee, one of a group of drivers waiting to be called upon. A large mirror on the wall also offered him a view of the roulette and baccarat tables. That would have to do.

Seen from behind, he noticed a tenseness in Onslow's shoulders. The young man showed nerves, after all.

'Frightfully sorry,' a familiar voice said as a splash of water hit Jack's hand. Reggie Fitzpatrick stood in front of him, in tails and white tie and with a glass of soda in his hand.

Jack gave him a bland smile.

'Nothing so far.' Fitzpatrick dried his own hand with a handkerchief.

'Maybe you've scared them off, if you've been recognised.'

'That's a risk I had to take. We simply don't have enough people otherwise.'

'What if they split up?'

'Mr Bernardo has orders to keep them at the baccarat table, and I have someone at the bar. See the girl?' A young woman with golden hair and a white satin dress that showed the maximum amount of skin permissible without being vulgar, sashayed into view. As if drawn by a magnet, Uncle Sal's companions turned to admire her.

'My niece. She's also my private secretary. None of them have ever met her, and she's using the name Colette for this occasion. I'll be in the ball room, if you need me.'

With a small nod, Fitzpatrick left Jack to his observation. He saw Uncle Sal wiggle one hand behind his back, a signal he had everything under control.

'D o you mind?' Colette showed her dimples as she squeezed in next to Uncle Sal. He promptly made space for her.

'But you are most welcome, Signorina. Can we offer you a drink?'

'How frightfully nice.' She offered Uncle Sal her hand. He bent over it and kissed it with all the exuberance his role demanded.

'I'll have a Cat-A-Tonic, Pierre,' she said to the bartender.

'What a delightful name,' Jordan said. 'Shall we have a round of those, gentlemen?'

'Right-ho,' Bassington-Whyte said. 'I mean, it sounds terribly delicious, Miss –'

Another dimpled smile rewarded him. 'Cobell, but please call me Colette. And you are?'

'Where are our manners? I'm Dominic Jordan, and these young oafs are Peter Onslow, Andrew Morris and Wilfred Bassington-Whyte. The gentleman to your other side is Mr Bernardo.' Jordan's teeth gleamed pearly white in the light from the chandelier. He flashed Onslow a triumphant grin as the young woman propped an elbow up on the bar and leant closer to him.

Their cocktails turned out to be pale green concoctions, with a hint of bitterness and a refreshing tartness. 'It's Pierre's own creation,' Colette said. 'He won't give anyone the recipe, although I won't give up. I have a few more nights where I can try.' She fluttered her blackened eyelashes at the bartender.

'If your smile isn't enough for Pierre, which it would be for me, have you attempted bribery?' Jordan asked.

Colette took another sip. Her lip rouge glistened. 'That's next on my list, as soon as I've struck it lucky at the baccarat table. Tonight's the night. I can feel it.'

'That's where we're heading.' Bassington-Whyte gulped down his cocktail. Uncle Sal decided to keep a close eye on him. In his experience, knocking back cocktails in that manner spoke of untold worries, not a taste for drink.

He caught Onslow watching his friends too. The young man glanced an awful lot at the door as well, when he thought he was unobserved, Uncle Sal thought. Was he sharing their suspicions? He'd have to be a blithering idiot not to put one and one together when the documents disappeared. In fact, all three of the men had to be smart enough to be working in Whitehall. They might not have Uncle Sal's own worldliness, or Jack's quick intelligence, and family connections accounted for a lot, yet the Empire wasn't run by fools.

Colette slipped off her bar stool. One hand clutched a beaded evening bag with a peacock feather design, the other reached for her cocktail.

'Allow me,' Morris said. He carried her drink to the baccarat table for her. Four of the seven seats were already taken.

'We could partner up,' Jordan suggested to her. 'But what about you, Mr Bernardo?'

Uncle Sal gingerly tested his gammy ankle. 'I shall be your mascot,' he said. 'I, and fortune, will smile upon you.' He snapped his fingers at a waiter as he arranged himself on a chair with a perfect view of the baccarat game.

The waiter asked for his wishes, and Uncle Sal instructed him to fetch Jack. As clever as Mr Fitzpatrick's niece had shown herself to be, Jack possessed the right skills to detect anything underhand when it came to gambling. And, as an artist, he had a knack for remembering faces, in case one of the men did manage to make contact with anyone.

The croupier put a large stack of red, blue and white gambling chips in front of Bassington-Whyte and Colette. Onslow and Morris settled on small stakes.

Jack strolled into the room, with the unobtrusive air of a man used to being invisible to his betters. Uncle Sal gave him an imperious wave. He'd decided that his character was used to having servants at his call.

'You wanted to see me, sir,' Jack said.

The roulette wheel spun, and the ball ended on the 23. Colette, who'd placed a fifty francs jeton on red, purred as she raked in her winnings. The gentlemen had bet on the wrong numbers and shrugged off their losses with good grace.

'Save my spot,' Onslow said as he rose.

'I need my pills. I forgot that Mrs Clifton has them in her purse,' Uncle Sal told Jack.

Jack had no trouble keeping up with Onslow, who made his way to the restrooms. He followed him inside and turned on the tap to wash his hands. The cubicle doors ended an inch above the floor. He glimpsed the top of Onslow's shoes in the mirror. The man in the next cubicle wore black-and-white wingtips. The other cubicles were empty.

Outside, a potted fern gave Jack enough cover to hide from view until Onslow and the man with the wingtips both left the restroom. Jack peeked around the plant to catch a glance at the man's features. Satisfied he'd remember the sallow face and square jaw, he left his place to continue his errand when he spotted Jordan in the door, signalling a doe-eyed cigarette girl.

During the drive to town, he'd offered his friends

smokes from a well-filled cigarette case, but Jack thought it likely that he was trying to flirt with the girl, who was as exquisite as her surroundings.

Aunt Mildred danced in the arms of an elderly gentleman who counted the foxtrot steps under his breath. Her placid expression had become frozen.

Lydia, a vision in a deep blue satin dress, matching gloves and diamond and sapphire jewellery flirted over a glass of champagne with a brilliantined man oozing Latin charm. Her friend Anne fanned herself. She had kept her dress simple by sticking to silver throughout, but her eyes sparkled, and her cheeks glowed as her partner led her towards a table.

Jack waited until the dance finished before he approached Aunt Mildred and asked her for the tablets.

She blinked at him before she gave a little laugh and rummaged in her evening bag. 'Remind Mr Bernardo not to take more than one per hour,' she instructed him as she handed over a pill box containing her breath mints.

In a nook, Fitzpatrick had claimed a place with his back to the wall. Nobody paid him any attention. Jack chuckled to himself. Despite their lack of men, they should be able to keep up their surveillance. What a pity Frances wasn't here with them. He wondered what she was doing.

Frances was thinking the same about Jack and Uncle Sal. She sat in the servants' room, where Geraldine read *Powder and Patch* by Georgette Heyer, and her eyes became rounder and rounder as she turned the pages.

Mrs Foster embroidered a handkerchief with Aunt Mildred's initials, and Frances found herself with nothing to do. She was arguing with herself whether she should run up and fetch her own book when the butler entered with Tinkerbell, who hurled himself at her in his delight to see her again.

'What a beautiful little dog,' she said. 'What's her name?'

'His name is Tinkerbell.' Mr Bowman pointed at stern finger at the corgi who gave him a reproachful woof as he sat on his hunches. 'He appears to like you.'

Frances stroked the soft fur and Tink sighed with delight. 'I hope so. Look at his sweet face.'

'In that case, you're welcome to take him for his walks,' Geraldine said. 'Last time, the little scamp spattered my new stockings with mud when he was digging up a flower bed.' Her gaze softened as Tink settled on Frances's feet. 'Mind you, he's a nice enough dog.'

'I'd love to take care of him,' Frances said. Walking Tink gave her a good excuse to leave the house, or to run into Jack. And she'd missed the cheerful little corgi who'd won their hearts during the sea voyage.

'Are you sure?' The butler gave her a quizzical glance.

'Too right I am,' she said.

Geraldine giggled. 'Do all Australians talk funny like you?'

Although Frances had intentionally stressed her heritage, because it gave her an excuse for any mistake she might make, the maid's reaction stung.

'Frances might think the same about you,' Mrs Foster said without missing a stitch on her embroidery. 'I recollect having to remind you about your aitches more than once.'

Geraldine scowled.

Frances took pity on her. 'I think you sound like a real lady, and I'd be grateful if you could teach me. I don't want to embarrass the mistress, or the household.'

'That's the spirit. If you put on your coat and stout shoes, I'll show you Tinkerbell's evening routine.' Mr Bowman gave her an encouraging nod, and Frances dashed upstairs.

The balmy night air was filled with a mixture of scents that Tink sniffed with relish. Frances held his leash while she strolled with the butler along the flagstone path. He illuminated their path with a flashlight.

'I hope you find the work acceptable,' he said when

they were at a safe distance from the house. 'We're well aware what we're asking from you.'

'I don't mind.' If he'd seen how the Palmers used to scrape every penny together and how much hard work Frances was used to, he'd probably goggle. Still, she enjoyed the idea of herself as a sheltered young lady who barely knew that grates didn't clean themselves and floors needed scrubbing.

'How much do you know about Geraldine's boyfriend?' she asked.

'I wasn't aware she had one.'

'Well, she does, back in London, and he lost his job. She's keen on him starting his own bakery if they can find the money, and to get married. His name is Bill.' A knot of dread formed in her stomach. 'You won't hold it against them if it turns out to be nothing?'

'Certainly not. It must be hard for you to spy on people, but in this case, we have no choice.'

Tinkerbell stopped and wagged his tail stub. 'What's wrong, Tink?' Frances asked.

The butler laughed. 'This is how he tells me he's been on his leash long enough.'

'Shall I let him run?'

'Not in the dark, I'm afraid. Madam is afraid he'll go down a rabbit-hole again, and we'd have our work cut out to spot him at night.'

'Sorry, Tink.' He rubbed himself against Frances's legs.

'Is there anything else?'

Frances told him about Anne's repaired clothing and Bassington-Whyte's gambling debts.

'That's interesting,' the butler said. 'I'll have our people check their bank accounts.'

'How do these things work? It's not good enough to simply steal documents like these unless you already have a buyer.'

'We were wondering about that too. The likeliest explanation is that the thief has either done this before and was told to keep his eyes open for an opportunity to purloin anything worthwhile, or he'd been recruited before.'

'It's an awfully slim chance to be in the right place, with such a small house party and staff.' That question had been niggling in the back of her mind all day.

'Not really. It's been fashionable for quite some time to spend the holiday period at the Cote d'Azur, and nobody would think twice if you run into all kinds of acquaintances. And they all move in the same circles, so word spreads.'

'We're not any closer, then?'

'I wouldn't say that. You've already unearthed some useful information, and who knows what our friends are discovering this very moment?'

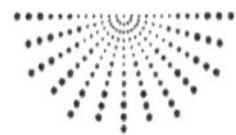

With every passing minute, Jack became more convinced they were wasting their time. He'd followed Onslow and Jordan outside, where they cooled off in the night air. Both men were ahead with their winnings, while Morris tended to bet with enough caution to stay in the game without losing. Bassington-Whyte's pockets had suffered. He'd tried to cover up his agitation, but Jack knew the signs by heart. Something rested heavily on the young man, and it couldn't be simply the loss of a few hundred francs.

Bassington-Whyte had given up on gambling and instead joined the ladies in the ball room, without making a stop on the way. Jack couldn't discount the possibility of a note changing hands in the crowded rooms, but he doubted the young man had the necessary dexterity, or the sanguinity. Even if the thief believed that Onslow had not noticed the loss of the documents, they'd burn under his nails.

The other three had cooler heads, as demonstrated at the card table. Contrary to Bassington-Whyte, they had only upped their stakes when the odds favoured them. Jack wondered if Onslow possessed any intelligence training. He kept his cool remarkably well, considering the circumstances. Only a slight twitch in his fingers betrayed his nerves as he struck a light for his cigarette.

Jordan leant on the balustrade next to him. 'Makes a nice change to escape the house for a while, and to see a few new faces.'

'I didn't know you were bored.' Onslow took a deep drag.

Jack moved as close as he could towards them, under cover of the overhanging roof.

'Don't tell me you weren't. It would be easier if Mrs Clifton had taken a villa in town or hired enough cars for a party.' Jordan took out his cigarette case and lit a gasper.

'You can always ring up for a taxi.' Jack detected a hint of amusement as Onslow continued, 'I assume your sudden desire for independence has nothing to do with the delightful Miss Cobell?'

'You must admit she's a remarkably pretty filly.'

'But without the pile of dosh your mother would insist upon.'

'Who said anything about marrying? All I'm saying is,

she's a pretty girl.' Jordan guffawed. 'Is that why you're distracted? Wedding bells on your mind?'

'Don't be an ass.' Onslow turned around, and Jack hurried to double back into the building. He had to dodge Lydia, who kept one hand clamped over the other wrist, as if somebody had hurt it. Her glance darted back and forth. Jack tried to catch a glimpse of anyone who might have followed her but could not see anyone suspicious.

One last glance through the doors told him that Lydia had not come to meet Onslow. She did not even seem to notice him, although he was less than ten feet away.

Jack did not dare linger any longer.

They drove home a little later. The young ladies dozed in the back, and Aunt Mildred too kept quiet.

A single light above the entrance stabbed the darkness as Jack switched off the headlights. A few hundred yards behind him followed the taxi with the men.

Bowman opened the door, as fresh looking at one in the morning as he'd been at noon.

'I hope Madam had a good night,' he said as he took the coats.

'Most pleasant. How is my little darling?'

'Tinkerbell is fast asleep, after his constitutional. The new maid was kind enough to take him out.'

'Good.' Aunt Mildred yawned. 'I'll have my morning tea at nine.'

J ack locked the car away and returned to the house, under the guise of serving as Uncle Sal's valet. 'Did you notice anything fishy?' Uncle Sal asked as Jack helped himself to a tot of brandy from the decanter on the side table. 'Apart from Bassington-Whyte's lack of a clear head, I mean? Do you think that's a sign of a heavy conscience?'

'Onslow made a few attempts to be on his own, but that could simply be because he's tired of the constant company. We should have asked when this party was organised. If the guest list existed before the rumours about the blueprints were spread, they would all seem a lot more harmless than they do otherwise.'

'True.' Uncle Sal rubbed his eyes. Sitting for hours observing unobtrusively had exhausted him.

'I'll see if I can catch up with Bowman and Frances in the morning,' Jack said. 'I'll keep you updated when I come to shave you.'

'I could get used to this,' Uncle Sal said. 'As long as you make sure my Frances is well looked after.'

'I will. At least for once we're not entangled in a murder case.'

T he cold from the stone floor sent a chill up Frances's stockinged legs. Outside, an owl hooted in the dark. She hurried to sweep away the ashes of last night's fire and light fresh logs. She warmed her hands over the flames. After such a balmy evening, the early morning chill came as unwelcome surprise.

The kettle whistled and the water in the copper made the pipes crackle merrily as the kitchen door inched open. Frances gave a start until she recognised the cook in her thick coat and muffler.

'Bonjour,' Madame Petit cast a probing glance over the floor, and her stove, and the array of tea trays set ready to be taken up at nine. She gave Frances a satisfied nod, unbuttoned her coat and hung it over a peg behind the door, together with her muffler. 'Coffee for us?'

Frances inhaled the heavenly aroma. Her stomach grumbled, but it wouldn't be too much longer before the rest of the staff came down for breakfast. Cook poured a generous amount of milk into her mug.

One sip of the brew, and Frances did the same. Cook chuckled at her expression. 'It is strong, non?'

'Very.' But it also awakened every nerve in her body.

The warmth from the fireplaces and the oven spread through the servants' room as Frances set the table. Dawn already streaked the sky orange and pink as she put out bread, butter and eggs.

'Good morning, miss,' Jack said with his sleepy grin.

Her heart skipped a beat. She beamed at him. 'Please, call me Frances.'

Geraldine rushed in, sliding the last pin into her neat

bun. 'Gosh, I'm starving.' Nevertheless, she kept standing until the butler and Foster had arrived and taken their accustomed places.

'How are you today?' the butler asked Frances. 'Madame Petit tells me she finds your work most satisfactory.'

Frances heaved a relieved sigh.

'What is going to happen tonight, Mr Bowman?' Geraldine asked. 'Are we having a New Year's party for the staff?'

'Madam has kindly consented to us going down to the promenade for a while.' He bestowed a kindly smile upon them. 'There's bound to be dancing, I'm told.'

'How smashing.' The maid clasped her chest. 'But how will we get there and back?'

'I'll take care of the transport.' Jack buttered his bread. 'I'm supposed to pick Mrs Clifton and her guests up at two in the morning, which gives everyone a chance to celebrate.'

'Where are they going to party? With us?'

Frances's innocent question earned her an exasperated eye-roll from Geraldine. 'Not likely, is it? I don't know about Australia, but here the gentry don't mix with the likes of us, and we wouldn't want them to.'

'Quite right.' Mrs Foster sipped her tea. She declined to try the strong coffee that Jack downed with relish. 'Although I'm not sure I'd call that Mr Bernardo gentry.'

Frances's skin prickled. 'Why do you say that?' she asked. 'He seems every inch the gentleman.'

'I shouldn't say anything.' The older woman concentrated on her food.

Mr Bowman jumped in. 'I'm sure whatever you say will not leave this room.'

A hint of distaste flickered over Mrs Foster's features. 'It's only that madam seemed not too happy to be asked to have him under her roof. She mentioned something about the late master having his doubts about Mr Bernardo, as charming as he may be.'

'She thinks he's a rotter? But what is there to gain here? Madam keeps her expensive jewellery at home, and Lady Bassington-Whyte's diamonds are mostly paste.' Geraldine smirked. 'She thinks nobody can tell.'

'Nothing of that sort.' Mrs Foster wagged a stern finger at her.

'I reckon there's a goodish bit of money to be made if you overhear the right kind of information from the right kind of people.' Jack grinned. 'Probably nothing but a rumour.'

'The late master wasn't the fanciful type, and neither is madam.'

'In which case Mr Bernardo would have long since been found out,' the butler said. 'I'd appreciate it if you kept your mistress's confidence from now on.'

'Did she really say that he's a bad hat?' Geraldine asked.

'That's enough about that, Geraldine. Don't forget your position.' Mr Bowman helped himself to more eggs.

Tommy sat outside the French doors, throwing a ball for Tinkerbell.

'Are you sure it was a wise idea to invite that Bernardo fellow?' Tommy asked his aunt in a plaintive tone designed to carry far enough to reach the company indoors.

Aunt Mildred frowned. 'Is there a problem?'

'Probably not, it's just, dash it, Aunt Mildred. In the Office, he's said to be a crafty fellow, one who isn't too picky when it comes to making money. They say he knows lots of people and even more secrets. I've heard rumours that practically say he stole an invention from a business partner and sold it to his foreign friends. And my uncle ...'

'Your uncle was perfectly well aware of Mr Bernardo's reputation.' Aunt Mildred lowered her voice enough to hint at deepest confidentiality. Still, eavesdroppers should be able to listen in without too much effort. 'I've been asked to include him in our little gathering.'

'Asked by whom?'

'By someone who is convinced that a man this ingenious will always keep his merchandise close at hand,

and that he would only accept my invitation if it could profit him. I won't say any more.'

'You mean, he's gotten hold of something else he wants to sell to the highest bidder? I've heard he's been frightfully friendly with a few people in the navy.'

'Keep your voice down and stop speculating. I expect you to treat Mr Bernardo as an honoured guest. If he is really up to no good, as they say in the pictures, the deal must take place or else the buyers will remain unknown. That's all I've been told and more than you needed to know.' She stroked Tink's head. 'Shall Tommy throw your ball again?'

Tommy flung the toy with all his might and the corgi dashed to chase it. 'Do you think we put it on too thick?' he murmured.

'No. If it were me, I'd do my outmost to figure out who Sal is dealing with and add them to my own list of buyers.' She put her hand in the crook of his elbow while they both watched the happy antics of the dog. They had cast their bait, and now the wait began.

CHAPTER EIGHT

The last evening of the old year went by in a frenzied rush for Frances. Jack had chauffeured first the gentlemen and then the ladies into town before he returned for the staff. While everyone else dressed in their fineries, Frances sprinkled a fine powder onto Uncle Sal's floorboards. She only covered the areas leading to his desk and his wardrobe.

Mr Fitzpatrick had promised them the powder would cling to shoes, or if any unwanted visitor went shoeless, to his socks. It would also form a trail which they would be able to follow with a torch. Should anyone feel the urge to search Uncle Sal's room, they could thus identify him.

Frances shone her own torch on her handiwork, to make sure she hadn't accidentally trod on the powder. Everything appeared fine. She switched the torch off again, making the powder invisible to the eye.

She still grinned to herself as she put on her own party frock, a well-cut pink satin dress. If she wasn't the guest of honour as planned, at least she could dazzle Jack and Uncle Sal.

The promenade in Nice shone with a thousand lights that glistened on the inky water. The palm fronds swayed in the night air. Jazz music wafted from the palais, where Aunt Mildred and her party celebrated. It competed with the French songs played by a small band on the square. Hundreds of revellers stood listening, and dancing. Jack and Frances had limited themselves to two dances, between turns he took with Geraldine and a delighted Foster.

Frances had also danced with Mr Bowman, who was almost as light on his feet as Jack.

There were no taxi cabs to be found near the pier, so none of the guests could sneak back to the villa. For once they could relax. Or at least, they would have been able to if not for having to pretend to be strangers. Frances's glance wandered to Jack. He gave her a tiny signal to follow him.

They met in a small alley, leading away from the square. Above them, a myriad of stars sparkled, and the heady scent of jasmine and mimosas sweetened the air despite the smoke from a few wood fires.

Frances slipped her hand into Jack's and leant her head against his shoulder. 'I wish we didn't have to hide.'

'We won't have to for much longer, if this plan works.'

'I hope so. Aunt Mildred is trying to hide it, but she's terribly worried. She nearly forgot to take Tink's toy along.'

'Which reminds me, I need to pick him up.'

Aunt Mildred had been adamant not to leave Tinkerbell on his own. If the thief worked with an accomplice, there might be an attempt at breaking into Uncle Sal's room while they were all gone. A criminal who saw himself confronted with a small dog, might become desperate.

Both Aunt Mildred and Tommy had decided to take turns when it came to looking after Tinkerbell. The dog also gave them a good excuse to stroll around and keep an eye on their suspects. Close to midnight though, there would be a terrible crush when all the society people came together. Jack had promised to take over Tinkerbell's care half an hour before. Because Frances's fondness for the corgi was well established, it was the most natural thing for them to walk Tink together.

The little dog spotted them from afar. His stubby tail wagged with a flattering enthusiasm as Tommy lifted him into Jack's arms. A sandy paw print marred the beauty of Tommy's white dinner jacket. He wiped at it with good-natured resignation.

Behind Tommy, golden light streamed out of a palais, and dozens of voices tried to make themselves heard over the music.

'Everything's clear so far,' he said. 'Although Morris claimed his oysters must have been bad and asked for a lift home.'

'Did he return to the villa?'

Tommy shook his head. 'Onslow went to fetch a taxi, but every car for hire was already booked up for the night. Aunt Mildred gave him a dose of bicarbonate of soda which seemed to settle his stomach.'

'Anyone else trying to give you the slip?'

'Nobody, but because of Morris's delicate condition, we've decided you take us home first and the girls last. That means, while you're gone again, I'm the only one watching over the house, because Uncle Sal can't be separated from Aunt Mildred.'

'You're not alone,' Frances said with a little more force than planned. 'Mr Bowman and I will be back.'

'True, but you can't guard Uncle Sal's room, whereas I can spy through my keyhole.' Tommy broke off as he heard someone call his name. 'Don't forget, Tinkerbell does not like ducks or geese. Stay away from the water with him.'

'Very well, sir.' Jack doffed his cap. Frances giggled as they strolled away with their canine charge.

She felt wide awake. Because of New Year's, breakfast would be two hours later than usual, and

Frances could stay in bed until seven. She intended to make the most of every precious moment with Jack.

At the stroke of midnight, the music fell silent, and all the church bells broke out into a jubilant peal, to ring in the new year. Their measured bongs echoed in the still air. Jack pulled Frances in for a long kiss that stifled every other thought in her. 'Happy 1932, my love,' he said.

'To us and to a happy new year.' She drank in every bit of this moment, the way Jack held her and gazed into her eyes, the way his sleepy blue eyes crinkled, and the beauty of the star-spangled moonlit night under a French sky. Her heart burst with happiness as they kissed again.

At ten past one in the morning, she danced into her room, with Tinkerbell cradled in her arms. Because Uncle Sal's room had no balcony, a thief would most likely come from inside the house. Nevertheless, Mr Bowman sat watch in the garden.

Tink snuggled onto the foot of Frances's bed as she changed into flannel pyjamas and a thick night-robe and sat by the window, waiting for Jack's return. She must have dozed off at one point, because the next thing she knew, Tink bumped his nose against her shin. On the floor below, doors fell to. She did the only sensible thing and went to bed.

The next morning, when Frances rose to prepare the breakfast table, there were no signs of a powder trail leading from Uncle Sal's room. Her heart sank, but then it had been a long shot anyway. Nevertheless, they decided to leave the trap in place. For Frances, it only meant no sweeping in Uncle Sal's room, and he had to take care where he stepped.

Everyone seemed tired this morning, she thought, as she dusted the ladies' bedrooms. A quick glance in Anne's wardrobe had confirmed Geraldine's hints. The clothes were carefully darned and updated, and the shoes had seen better days.

Lydia's possessions were more expensive and newer, but her jewellery case contained surprisingly little. This, and her brother's unease and gambling losses put the Bassington-Whytes firmly on the list of suspects.

Outside, the Chevrolet rolled up to the house. Frances opened the window of Lydia's bedroom and shook out her duster. Somewhere else she heard another window open as Bowman stepped out to meet Jack.

'Mr Bernardo will be ready in five minutes,' the butler said. 'While you're in town, Madam asks you to pick up a delivery of wine.'

'On New Year's Day?'

'The merchant lives above his shop.' Bowman slipped a note into Jack's hand.

The other window was closed again. Frances followed suit as soon as she saw Uncle Sal head outside.

A rap on Lydia's door startled her.

'Hurry up,' Geraldine called.

Frances snatched her duster and polish and rushed to the door. The maid shook her head at her. 'I swear I have never seen anything like it.'

'Am I that slow?'

'Gosh, no. But that Mr Bernardo rushing off has them all in a tizzy. Cook says they were fairly flying through breakfast, and that with her making fresh pastries and all.' Geraldine leant in, to Frances. 'I bet it's because they all think he's fishy as Billingsgate.'

'Gosh.'

'Oh, and I'm to tell you Mr Morris is unwell, and you don't need to do his room.'

Interesting, Frances thought as Geraldine flitted off. The man must either be really ill, or he wanted an excuse to stay behind when the rest of the party went out. Aunt Mildred had arranged for tennis, and a picnic in the orangerie for the afternoon.

In Wilfred Bassington-Whyte's room, she cast a longing glance at the locked drawer. The other gentlemen left theirs conveniently open. The only locked items there were their trunks on top of the wardrobe. Bowman would need to keep Geraldine and Foster busy if Frances should ever have the opportunity to have a proper snoop.

She tidied the bedrooms automatically, while mulling

over the situation. Neither she nor Jack had as much liberty as they needed, and Uncle Sal's every step in the villa was watched by people. Why didn't Mr Fitzpatrick take a closer look at everybody's finances before the theft, and before all the banks closed for the holidays? Jack thought it had to do with a sense of fair play and a lack of an excuse when no crime had happened yet.

To Frances, that sounded barmy. Surely Mr Fitzpatrick would be discreet and come up with a convincing story for the bank managers.

A coy giggle made her stop as she was about to leave the last bedroom. She hurried to return inside and close the door until only a tiny gap remained.

A few words reached her ears. ' … mind? That …… risk.' A high-pitched female voice. Frances crouched and glimpsed through the gap. A pair of black shoes with sensible heels. Geraldine, then. Now a man spoke in hushed tones. ' …worth your while.'

Footsteps retreated into different directions. Frances pushed herself off the floor. The maid, in cahoots with a man. Her heart sang, despite her disappointment. She didn't want Geraldine to be a criminal, but the idea of solving the case for Aunt Mildred's sake cheered her up no end. All they needed to do was to find out which of the gentlemen had hired Geraldine to do something for him. Maybe she'd kept the documents safe or handed them over to someone else in the guise of a delivery man or another person nobody would notice.

Frances flew down the staircase and knocked a folded rug out of Mr Bowman's arms. 'Careful,' he said. She dropped her voice to a whisper as she picked up the rug. 'I'm so sorry.'

'We're alone,' he said. 'I assume you've got something to tell me.'

His face grew grave as she told him. 'That means we need to keep an eye on the girl, and we're already stretched.'

'But the other person?'

Mr Bowman sighed. 'Could have been anyone. Most days the gentlemen play pool for a bit or lounge around in the games room, and I have no reason to enter it.'

'Ask Tommy,' she said. 'He would have noticed if someone excused himself. If nobody did, there's only Mr Morris left.'

The door to the staircase opened from below. Frances hurried down.

In the hours until the party left the house for tennis, first cook and then Mr Bowman kept her rushed off her feet. No wonder most households had so many servants, she thought, as she polished the silverware. At this rate, she could consider herself lucky if she could break into that dratted drawer at all.

Geraldine strutted past her in the kitchen, with a big pout on her face. 'You wouldn't believe it,' she said. 'Mr Tommy just had to go and let that dog jump all up and down on him, and who is it has to make sure there won't be any stains left?'

'Oh, no. I'd offer to help you, but –' Frances pointed at the silverware still waiting for her ministrations. 'What about Mrs Foster?'

The pout deepened. 'She's busy mending madam's dress. How anyone can tear a hole in a lace collar is beyond me.'

A chuckle escaped Frances as Geraldine flounced off, towards the butler's pantry. Cook had the afternoon off, so it should be safe to sneak upstairs in a few minutes.

A few minutes later, her jaw dropped as she saw the large, sealed envelope Wilfred Bassington-Whyte had hidden away in his drawer.

CHAPTER NINE

Frances turned the thick envelope over and over in her hands. She didn't dare break the gummed flap. If only Jack was back, but he and Uncle Sal intended to stay out until dinner to give their thief the chance to break into the room.

What if she simply took the envelope? Too risky, she told herself. If Bassington-Whyte discovered his loss, he was bound to destroy any evidence that might lead them to his paymasters.

She had no choice but to put it back where she found it. Next on her list came Dominic Jordan's room, although she felt inclined to stop her search after this discovery and leave the rest to Mr Bowman and Mr Fitzpatrick.

The thud of feet on the marble staircase warned her just as she turned the handle.

Her mouth went dry as she gripped the feather duster

she had brought as an alibi. Frances stretched onto her tiptoes to clean the top of the doorframes as Mr Onslow came in sight, in grass-stained flannels.

His fair face appeared slightly flushed as he spotted her. Frances lowered her gaze and wielded her duster with all the concentration she could muster.

Ten minutes later, she straightened the sheet on Mr Jordan's bed as her fingers touched something stiff. She slipped her hand deeper under the mattress and pulled out a magazine. She dropped it as soon as she took in the cover. No wonder the young man kept this particular reading (or more likely ogling) material hidden from plain view. Frances didn't consider herself especially prudish, but she'd never seen a magazine with a female on the cover whose physical charms were only hidden by a few strategically placed tassels.

The magazine went back into its original place. Frances barely had time to finish with the bed before the door flew open and Geraldine tugged Frances by the arm. 'This can wait,' she said, catching her breath. 'We're both needed in the kitchen. Honestly, we're that rushed off our feet in this house, and on New Year's Day too.'

Madame Petit pouted as Frances rushed in. 'See this.' She held up a dead pheasant by its neck.

Frances gave her a puzzled look.

'It has to be naked. All naked.' The cook pointed with a flourish to three more very much not plucked pheasants. 'They need …' She tore out a feather for demonstration.

'I'll take care of it,' Frances said with a sinking heart. In Mr Wodehouse's world, servants shimmered to and fro, but there never were unsuspecting housemaids who'd originally been invited as guest of honour, reduced to poultry plucking.

'Not in here.' Madame Petit shooed her and Geraldine out. 'Feathers, they fly, and fly.' Considering the simmering pots on the stove, Frances had to agree.

'Shall we pluck them outside?' she asked Geraldine who stared at her as if she were barmy, no, daft.

'And have those ruddy feathers go everywhere? It's that windy outside.' As if to emphasise her words, leaves blew against the kitchen window. 'We'll have to use the butler's pantry.'

They bundled up the game birds in a piece of sacking and carried them between them. Geraldine pinched her nose, although the pheasants did not smell.

Mr Bowman crossed their path carrying a silver drinks tray. He gave Frances a tiny shrug, as if to acknowledge their difficulties.

There was no lunch today for the staff except for a few sandwiches Foster brought them. The pheasants proved themselves to be tough adversaries. Frances, who had only plucked chickens before, and that on rare occasions, could have despaired over the task. As if it weren't bad enough that her fingers ached, every few minutes she crawled around and swept up the feathers that had escaped

Geraldine. At this rate, she would never be able to talk to the butler in privacy.

A bell rang. And then again. Geraldine bit her lip. 'It's Lady Bassington-Whyte. Do you think Foster will answer it?'

'Not if she's busy with Au –' Frances scolded herself. She almost said Aunt Mildred. 'Our mistress.' If Geraldine had noticed the slip, she would claim it was the Aussie accent that sounded weird.

The bell rang again. Geraldine wiped her hands and jumped up, distributing yet another load of feathers on the floor.

'Go and wash, I'll clean this up.' Frances sighed.

Geraldine grabbed the bar of soap next to the sink in the corner.

'Finally, alone,' Frances muttered under her breath as soon as the maid was gone. She had lost all sense of time.

'I'm very sorry.' Mr Bowman poked his head through the door. He raised his eyebrows in an unspoken question.

She nodded, and he eagerly joined her. Despite being alone with him, Frances kept her voice to a whisper. 'There's a thick envelope in Mr Bassington-Whyte's locked drawer,' she said. 'It's this size.'

She spread out her hands to illustrate the dimensions, unsure if they were important or if blueprints could be folded again and again without causing any damage.

'That's promising,' he said. 'With any luck, it's

enough to make another push for financial records. Anything else that struck you as out of the order?'

Her cheeks grew warm. 'I didn't have much chance to snoop around,' she said, indicating the pesky game birds on the table. 'And it's probably nothing, but Mr Jordan keeps a, well, delicate magazine under his mattress. I mean, of a special nature.'

The corners of Mr Bowman's mouth curled up. 'True to a certain type, is he? Although it is interesting that the staff seeing it would embarrass him. Usually servants are considered invisible.'

'Or he is expecting other visitors.' Frances remembered the covert glances the young man had cast at Lydia and Anne.

The bell rang again, this time from the kitchen. 'I need to get these birds to Cook,' Frances said.

He held the door open as she wrapped up the poultry and put them in a large wicker basket. Her arms strained under the weight. On the way here, at least Geraldine had helped.

Jack and Uncle Sal returned just in time for the servant's dinner, a hasty meal consisting of grilled chops and roast potatoes, and a leftover trifle.

Ravenous though she was, Frances had to force herself to concentrate on the food. Jack had regaled them with descriptions of the town's sedated state after last night's celebrations, but that was all. If only she could catch him and Uncle Sal for a meeting. At least she should be free for the rest of the evening, whereas their ladies were sure to keep Foster and Geraldine busy.

Jack excused himself together with the ladies maids. He made a show of straightening his jacket. Frances's heart beat quickened. His pockets were obviously empty, although he always kept a cigarette lighter in them. He had sent her a message.

Frances stacked the dishes as she spotted Jack's lighter under his chair. She dropped to her knees and picked it up.

'Goodness,' she said, feigning surprise. 'I'll take this to Mr Sullivan. He'll be so worried when he can't find it.'

'Better hurry,' Mr Bowman said. 'There'll be dishes to be done soon.' His eyes held a trace of regret. 'We hired a girl for tonight, but in this weather, nobody will venture out.'

Madame Petit knitted her brows together. 'Geraldine shall help me.'

'I don't mind,' Frances said. 'That is, if I can take care of my other dress first. One of the pheasants was a bit ...' She left the rest of the sentence to their imagination.

'Salt, and baking soda.' The cook heaved herself upright, tired after an exhausting day.

Frances nodded obediently and slipped out of the room.

The wind blew her hair in her face as she opened the door. She reeled back. The sky had gone pitch black, and she thought she heard a faint rumble in the air. Stout boots and her coat were in order even for the short way to the garage.

Jack must have expected her because he flung the door wide open the second she set foot in front of it.

A small heater made his room cosy. She basked in the warmth, surprised at how cutting the wind had become, and snuggled into his arms. 'Your lighter is in my left coat pocket,' she said, unwilling to move.

He pressed a kiss on her hair. 'You're the cleverest girl I've ever met.'

A happy chuckle rose in her throat. 'You're not too bad either. So, what did you do today while I was knee-deep in poultry?'

Frances listened with envy as Jack mentioned a trip over the border to Italy. They had bought a *Corriere della Sera* to emphasise the fact that Mr Bernardo was in fact Italian, and that said country and with it unnamed purchasers of whatever Uncle Sal had to offer, were within easy reach.

'We'd better go back,' Jack said. 'Uncle Sal will need my valeting services, and it might be suspicious if you stay with me for too long.'

She pulled a face as he changed from his chauffeur's jacket into a dress jacket suitable for a gentleman's gentleman. Funny term, that. It was never a lady's lady, though. How unfair.

Jack tapped her nose and helped her into her coat. 'When this is over, can we go for a long drive?' she asked.

'Just you and me, I mean. No Uncle Sal, no Aunt Mildred.'

'What about Tinkerbell?'

She pondered. 'No. I don't want to share you even for a single moment.'

'Sounds good to me.'

Her knees grew weak as he pulled her close for a kiss.

'I 've been waiting.' Uncle Sal managed to arrange his five-foot nine frame into a towering posture.

'I'm sorry, sir.' Jack hung his head as he entered. Uncle Sal steered him clear of the desk, and the powder trail Frances had laid.

'It worked,' he said. Elation radiated off him and infected Jack.

'Your desk has been searched?'

'And the joker did a thorough job of it. All the hairs we put in between the different sheets of paper are gone, and the whole stash has been moved about an inch.'

'Someone with a professional eye for the original arrangement.'

'Too right. Now you only need to find out where the trail leads while I'm at dinner.'

Jack brushed off Uncle Sal's jacket and helped him down the stairs. The limp was very much on display as they parted ways outside the dining room.

'Mr Bernardo.' Uncle Sal kissed Aunt Mildred's hand, using the opportunity to glance under his lashes at the assembled guests.

Lady Bassington-Whyte looked flustered. Her son's face was flushed, while his sister simpered. Her friend Lydia studiously gazed anywhere but at young Bassington-Whyte. Morris, who'd been so unwell lately, had made a remarkably recovery. Although his hand travelled to his stomach whenever he felt watched, his eyes were clear and his skin rosy.

Uncle Sal righted himself and took a geek at Jordan and Onslow, who stood next to each other at the head of the table, ready to spring into action and lead the ladies to their seats. They tried to appear at ease, but Uncle Sal caught the same kind of tension between them he had encountered backstage, when competing actors pretended to be the best of friends while praying for the other one to make a fool of themselves. Which of the young ladies was the reason for the rivalry? He could have sworn that Miss Colette had made quite a splash with them, but it could just as well be Lydia or Anne.

The butler stood ready, waiting for the signal to serve the soup that stood ready on a trolley.

Tommy dashed into the room. 'Please forgive my tardiness,' he said with an unusual formality.

Aunt Mildred raised her pince-nez. 'Is there anything the matter?'

He gave her a sheepish grin. 'Tink's fine. It's just that

I spotted a newspaper in the library, and before I knew it, there was the dinner gong. Dashed interesting paper though.'

'On New Year's Day? It must have been days old.' She nodded to Bowman, who ladled a clear broth into soup bowls.

Tommy took his seat next to Lady Bassington-Whyte. 'That's it. It was today's edition, a *Corriere della Sera.*'

'That was mine.' Uncle Sal gave him a probing glance. 'I didn't know you speak Italian.'

'I don't. Just piecing things together from the old Latin.' Tommy tapped his head.

'I didn't know you can buy them in Nice,' Anne said.

'Who cares? Rely on English papers, and you'll know what's really going on.' Bassington-Whyte tucked in.

'I did not purchase my newspaper in France. We took a delightful tour into la bellissima Italia. Less than an hour, and the roads are surprisingly good, says your chauffeur.'

Someone sucked in their breath.

'I might have to borrow Sullivan again,' Uncle Sal said. He hoped that Bowman could study everyone's reactions.

'Of course,' Uncle Mildred said after a nervous pause. Uncle Sal admired her acting skills. She conveyed just the right mix of social hostess skill and an underlying distrust of his person. 'May I ask when?'

'In my experience things can never be said in advance.'

Bowman plated up pheasant, and the group fell silent.

Frances thought Aunt Mildred's dinner would never end. She'd wiped and dried the dishes from three courses already, and they were still not done. Add to that Geraldine and Foster, who were out and about everywhere in the house, while they waited for the ladies to demand their services, and it was impossible for her to follow the hopefully visible trail from Uncle Sal's room.

Her fingers twitched. A cup slipped out of her grip.

'Enough,' Jack said as he caught it. Instead of taking a well-earned break, he had offered his help too.

'I make coffee.' Madame Petit massaged her reddened hands. 'Or tea for you?'

'Coffee, please.' Jack flashed her a smile. 'Yours is the best I've ever tasted. And then you should get some well-earned rest. We can easily finish up.'

The cook heaved a sigh of relief. 'Merci.'

With Madame Petit out of the way, all Frances and Jack had to do was wait until the ladies went upstairs, with Foster and Geraldine to assist them with undressing. Tommy had received orders to keep the men occupied in the games room.

The butler's bell rang twice. 'Our signal,' Frances

whispered. Jack handed her a torch and tested his own. Together, they tiptoed up the servants' staircase, only to split up on the first floor. If somebody went wrong and they were spotted, Jack's presence outside Uncle Sal's room could be explained, just like Frances could make up an excuse for being in the hallway above them, where the others resided.

All was peaceful as she snuck onto the landing. She shone her torch onto the floor, while she strained to hear anything that signalled somebody coming. But the only sounds apart from her breath were Lady Bassington-Whyte's muffled promises to her daughter next door that she would send the maid over to darling Lydia in just a tic.

Frances hurried up. The light caught on a luminescent speck. And another one and another one. Together they formed a faint footprint, leading directly to a door.

In her happiness, she blew out her breath, only to regret it instantly. She switched off the torch and stole back down the servants' staircase, where Jack awaited her.

His eyes gleamed. 'A doozy of a trail if I ever saw one,' he said. 'No detour to another room or anything, just coming straight up towards the stairs.'

'On my end too,' she said.

'We got him? Who was it?'

She whispered a name in his ear.

CHAPTER TEN

'Peter Onslow?' Mr Bowman's eyes clouded over. They sat together in the butler's pantry, which he'd locked from inside. Outside, rain lashed the windows like billy-oh, and the wind howled. Frances nursed a tot of brandy. For now, it would help keep her awake, and later, to fall asleep. Jack had declined a drink.

'You never suspected him?'

'We suspected everyone. But I can't deny that I am surprised.'

'It makes sense,' Jack said. 'He had the best opportunity. It was his job to verify the blueprints, right?'

A grim nod from Bowman.

'And with the borders of Italy and Monaco so close, it's easier to meet here with a stranger than in London where you're bound to be spotted by the wrong person.'

Jack rubbed his chin, pensively. 'He'd also be the best equipped to see if Uncle Sal's material is the real thing. Plus, by raising the hue and cry with Fitzpatrick, he appeared to be lily-white. My guess is, he traded the blueprints first, before he did that.'

'But he didn't take anything from Uncle Sal's desk,' Frances said.

'He wouldn't, not before he has contacted his buyer, and he'd be crazy to go out on a foul night like this.' Jack sounded rueful.

'We must inform Mr Fitzpatrick.' Bowman helped himself to a stiff whisky. 'And we can't use the house telephone, in case somebody is nosey.'

'Which is why I hope you'll save me a bit from that whisky bottle. I'll need it after a bicycle ride in this weather.'

Frances cried out in alarm. 'You can't do that.'

'We have no choice.' Jack's warm hand clasped hers.

'Why can't Mr Bowman do it?' she pleaded.

'I would, Frances,' the butler said. 'But if I'm being summoned and I'm not around, there will be a big hullabaloo.'

'Then at least take the car.'

With infinite regret, Jack shook his head. 'The engine is too loud when she starts, and I have no reason to be out and about. It has to be the bicycle.'

Frances knew when she was beaten. 'What if Mr

Onslow has noticed that the stuff in Uncle Sal's drawer is fake, and makes a run for it?'

'He won't. I'll make sure of it.' Jack stroked her cheek. 'Don't worry. It'll be alright.'

The rain pummelled him without mercy as he sprinted towards the garage. He opened the hood of the Chevrolet and unscrewed the distributor cap. He shoved it into the toolbox, only to change his mind and hide the cap under a stack of old horse blankets in a corner. Nobody would be able to take the car out now.

Jack tightened his coat belt and pulled up the collar. Nothing for it then but to hop onto his bicycle and ride to the telephone box. He prayed that Fitzpatrick's hotel kept a concierge on duty at night.

Frances pressed her nose against her window, hoping against her better judgement to catch a glimpse of light from the garage signalling Jack's safe return. The storm had calmed down and the rain, though still heavy, no longer fell in impenetrable sheets. She hoped Jack's coat and boots had kept him dry.

She checked her small alarm clock. Past one already, and she had to be up in a few hours. Staring into the night wouldn't change that. She huddled under her blanket and willed herself to sleep.

The storm had died down completely by morning. Rain still glistened on the ground, and small runnels of water ran towards lower ground. A few bushes and palm trees were the worse for wear as Frances took out a bucket with the ashes, but the first traces of pink and orange flecked the sky.

Jack left the garage and came towards her.

'Good morning, kiddo,' he said and took the by now empty bucket from her.

He could have managed only a few hours of sleep and yet he looked as fresh as always. Frances rubbed her tired eyes. She wished she'd put on a dash of powder, to cover the dark shadows under her eyes.

Mr Bowman had also risen early. He awaited them in the butler's pantry, with a pot of tea so strong it would crinkle paint. Frances stirred two spoons full of sugar into hers and sipped with relish.

'How did it go?' he asked Jack as he handed him a mug of tea.

'Your boss-cockie will send for Onslow after breakfast and we're to pack up his belongings.'

'Why don't they come here to arrest him?' Frances asked.

'Because there's no real proof yet, and because we still want to keep the whole affair under wraps,' Mr

Bowman said. 'I assume Mr Fitzpatrick will cite a family emergency.'

'That's the plan. He's still working on the financial reports, but it seems that Lady Bassington-Whyte has drained the already straitened family finances, and her son is trying to dig them out of that hole with reckless gambling.' Jack rolled his eyes. 'Anne Deringham is also one of the newly poor which means it's not out of the question that Onslow worked hand in glove with someone else in the house.'

'And the others?'

'Nothing yet. Hopefully, Onslow will spill the beans when he's confronted with the facts.'

Their hopes were in vain. An hour later, after Frances had peeled and scraped enough potatoes and carrots to feed an army, Madame Petit took out the scraps. She emptied them into a basket to take home for her two pigs and went around the back of the house to smoke one of her cigarettes.

A few moments later her screams made Frances and Jack run out of the house.

Madame Petit pointed wordlessly at the marble staircase. At its bottom, half hidden by a spindly branch from a palm tree, two legs stuck out.

'Call a doctor and get Mr Bowman,' Jack said. He did not wait for an answer as he made his way down to the sorry sight. He already knew what to expect. Peter Onslow would not get the chance to spill any beans, ever again.

CHAPTER ELEVEN

After a cursory examination, Docteur Durand, a small man with a drooping moustache and melancholy eyes, told Jack and Mr Bowman to lift the body onto a stretcher and carry it into the garage.

Jack silently applauded his tact. Rich people tended to be displeased with being inconvenienced by the presence of a dead man, and he wouldn't put it past Lady Bassington-Whyte and the younger ladies to have a bout of hysterics over poor Onslow.

As for the doctor's verdict itself, Jack did not approve.

'It's obvious, non,' the doctor said. He picked up the wet branch and poked with it at a bundle of broken palm fronds strewn over the marble stairs. 'The young monsieur comes outside, maybe to have a smoke, maybe to gaze at the stars, he slips on the wet leaves, and down he goes on the slick marble. You will notice his neck is broken and

there is a gash on his forehead. Very unfortunate.' Dr
Durand sucked in air through his teeth. 'Let's get him
under a roof.'

They solemnly carried the body inside and lowered
the stretcher onto the ground. A chill ran over Jack's spine
as he gently covered the dead man with a clean blanket he
had fetched from his room. Jack said nothing but he had
decided he would stay with the body until Fitzpatrick
arrived or another person took charge of the case.

For Jack had noticed a detail the French doctor had
missed. While Onslow's neck was indeed broken, there
was a small bruise underneath his right ear. Someone had
struck him from behind with a cosh or a sandbag and then
killed him. Peter Onslow had been murdered.

'Dead?' Aunt Mildred grabbed the door jamb to
steady herself.

'I'm afraid so,' Mr Bowman said. 'I have asked the
doctor to wait in the library.' He gave her a reassuring
smile.

'An accident?'

'The doctor thinks he slipped on wet leaves.' Despite
these words, the butler shook his head, no.

'I see.' Aunt Mildred pressed a hand on her forehead.
'Is there anything left for me to do?'

'With your permission, I'd like to send Sullivan out to

purchase black armbands and take care of the other things.'

He kept his voice low and pleasant. Tinkerbell nevertheless proved himself to be susceptible to the heavy atmosphere and rubbed himself against Aunt Mildred's legs. She wrapped her dressing gown tighter around her and picked up the corgi. 'Of course. I assume it's best not to mention anything before breakfast.'

Mr Bowman inclined his head. 'Very well, Madam.'

As soon as he had left, she knocked on Tommy's adjoining door and bade him wake Uncle Sal. They needed to talk.

One glance at her pale face, and Uncle Sal knew something was up. 'What's wrong? It's not …' He pointed upstairs, meaning Frances.

'No, they're fine. It's Mr Onslow.'

'Peter?' Tommy's mouth fell open. 'Do you mean he's the rotter?'

Aunt Mildred put a finger on her lips. 'That was the original idea, from what little I know, but now I am no longer sure. You see, he's dead and Bowman thinks it was foul play.'

Foul play, Uncle Sal thought. When they'd first met, there had been a murder and she didn't shy away from the word. Now, under her own, if rented, roof, she couldn't bring herself to say so. 'Foul play' made it sound more palatable, as if the culprit had been naughty and cheated on the cricket field.

'We should call Jack,' Uncle Sal said. 'No flies on him. Best head on a man I've ever met.'

'He's staying with the body.' Aunt Mildred shut her eyes for a moment. Tink licked her hand. 'In case there's an attempt at tampering.'

'Where is Onslow's body?' Tommy' normally rosy cheeks had grown pale.

'In the garage.'

'I'll go down there and tell him to lock the place up. It would seem funny if he doesn't help Uncle Sal get ready.'

Aunt Mildred gazed after her nephew with a sense of helpless sympathy. 'I wish we were all out of this.'

Uncle Sal took her hand and gave it a light squeeze. 'We'll soon be, don't you worry.'

'But what if there's another murder?' She swallowed hard. 'What if you're next in line?'

'You worry too much. I'm not that easy to get rid of. Ask any old joker who tried to get my place in the billing order.' He saw with relief that a tiny twinkle crossed her face.

Because breakfast was an informal affair, available between nine and ten, the members of the house party ambled in at intervals. It gave Aunt Mildred opportunity to recover her composure. Uncle Sal sat opposite her, so they could observe every person as they entered the room. Bowman busied himself with bringing in hot and cold dishes, as the first two guests came in.

Bassington-Whyte's eyelids drooped, and his

shoulders sagged a little, until he noticed Aunt Mildred's eyes on him. He gave her a wan smile. 'Beastly night, that.'

His friend Jordan slapped him on the shoulder. 'If you insist on gong to bed without your nightcap, it is no wonder you couldn't sleep. Look at our lovely hostess and Mr Bernardo, both fresh as daisies.' He bent over Aunt Mildred's hand.

Uncle Sal made a mental note of Bassington-Whyte's unusual abstinence. Did he want to stay awake to slip out for a meeting with Peter Onslow, a meeting with a deadly ending? He itched to sit down for a decent chin-wag with his friends. What Jack had told them pointed to a clever and ruthless adversary. Did any of these spoilt young men have the brains for it?

The next arrivals interrupted his train of thoughts. He had been offered little occasion to become better acquainted with Morris, who held the door open for the ladies. Tommy traipsed in last, with Tink by his side.

'I hope there's a sausage or two left for us,' Tommy said. Uncle Sal approved of his acting skills. Nobody would have suspected that he had just marched past the body of a friend to fetch Jack.

Morris appeared chipper too, with a slight swagger in his step. The self-confidence of a man who had staged the perfect murder, maybe? And what about the women? Although Uncle Sal had trouble seeing any of them coshing a grown man and breaking his neck, Onslow wouldn't be the first one to fall for the promise of a secret rendezvous. If Lydia or Anne had acted as bait, their accomplice would have known where to lie in wait.

He banged his knife on the plate. If Onslow had been killed during the rain, the murderer would have gotten wet. His clothes might still be damp.

He cut off a large piece of bacon and let it slip off his fork, onto his lap. 'How stupid,' he said in a vexed tone. He rose. 'I shall return in a minute,' he said. 'Please keep my place for me.'

Just in time he remembered that Mr Bernardo had a heavy limp that might be heard outside the room, so he took his sweet time, despite his urge to hurry. He needed Frances or Jack, now.

Jack stood guard outside Onslow's door. They had locked it, and Jack kept the key in his pocket, but there was no guarantee that they were the only ones in the house who could pick locks. If any of the servants was involved, having the guests at breakfast gave them the perfect opening to search the room.

'Where's Frances?' Uncle Sal whispered.

'Tidying the young ladies' rooms. Why?'

Uncle Sal told him about his idea with the clothes. Jack thought back to the body. He had lifted Onslow's shoulders. The front of the coat had been damp, where the young man had lain face-down on the wet staircase. Had the back been wet as well? He couldn't say for sure. He closed his eyes to remember the details. 'He might have died after the rain,' he said. 'The face and neck had just started to stiffen, and the cold would have slowed down that process.'

Uncle Sal nodded. Jack had seen enough death during the Great Stoush to make him an expert. 'It's still worth a try,' he said and went to find Frances.

CHAPTER TWELVE

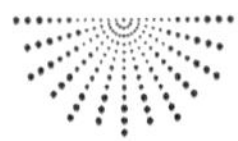

Raised eyebrows told Uncle Sal he'd been gone for longer than planned. Still, Mr Bernardo was never one to explain himself. Even better, the murderer might wonder what he had been up to. If the killer was in this room.

'Is Mr Onslow still not up?' Lady Bassington-Whyte's lips turned into a narrow crimson line in her heavily powdered face. 'I honestly don't understand what this generation is coming to.'

Aunt Mildred clasped her hands together and rose. 'Could I have your attention, please?'

Tommy's fork paused halfway to his mouth. Jordan and Morris put down their cups. Lady Bassington-Whyte's gaze travelled from her son to her daughter and back. Lydia giggled with Anne until her mother hissed at her.

'I'm afraid there has been an unfortunate accident,' Aunt Mildred said.

'An accident?' Lady Bassington-Whyte's forehead creased.

'Mr Onslow slipped outside, it appears on wet fronds, and fell down the staircase.'

Uncle Sal watched the group's reactions. Did he imagine the sound of an expelled breath?

All other eyes were on Aunt Mildred, ranging from bewilderment – Mrs Bassingon-Whyte and her daughter – to shock from Anne and Jordan, and disbelief from Tommy and Morris.

'Is he – I mean, shouldn't there be a doctor, and an ambulance?' Tommy asked.

'The doctor has already been here. I'm sorry to say there was nothing left for him to do.'

Uncle Sal made the sign of the cross.

Lydia's hand flew in front of her mouth. She bolted from the room.

Anne's gaze met with Bassington-Whyte's.

Morris's hands trembled, and Jordan clenched his. Uncle Sal wondered if they had ever encountered death before. Sure, they would have lost family members or older acquaintances in the war, but that did not compare to the knowledge that a man your own age, a friend, had lost his life not far from where they now sat over bacon, eggs, and toast.

Mrs Bassington-White fretted. 'Poor Lydia is so sensitive. Maybe I should follow her?'

Aunt Mildred said, 'Of course.'

'What happens now?' Jordan asked. 'Is he –'

'The body is in the garage.' Aunt Mildred took a deep, steadying breath. 'I've asked the maid to pack up his belongings. I need to inform his family. Do you have a name or an address for me?'

'Doesn't – didn't he have a sister at a boarding school, and an elderly aunt?' Jordan looked to Morris for help.

'I think so. The parents are dead. The Spanish Flu, if I remember correctly.' Morris nodded as if to confirm his own words. 'You should ring up Whitehall. They would have all the information.'

'If there's anything we can do to help you?' Jordan rested his forehead in his hand. 'To think that only last night we had a bit of an argument.'

'Did you? I thought I'd seen you stick your heads together,' Morris said.

'He warned me of being too chummy with strangers. I took it he wanted me to back off charming the beautiful Miss Cobell.' Jordan attempted a brave grin. 'And today he's gone, forever. I wish we could help in any way, Mrs Clifton. Or, if you'd rather we leave?'

'No. Nonsense.' Aunt Mildred reached for her coffee and took a sip. She pulled a face and rang the bell.

Bowman slipped into the room. 'Madam?'

'Fresh coffee, please.' She addressed her guests. 'As sad as this tragic accident is, life must go on. We shall change our programme a little, of course, but I am convinced Mr Onslow would have wanted us all to be merry.'

'And it would be difficult to change the travel arrangements,' Tommy said.

'Then it's all set. We'll stay.' Bassington-Whyte still held his gaze fixed on Anne.

Frances abandoned the dusting in Lydia Bassington-Whyte's room and opened the wardrobe. She felt the shoulders of the coat. They were dry. There was a coat rack in the cloakroom downstairs, but she couldn't risk abandoning her duties upstairs, and she hoped that Uncle Sal would manage to give butler the message that he needed to check the garments there.

She closed the wardrobe and went next door, just as Lydia staggered up the staircase.

More steps, and high-pitched voices alerted her, although even with her ear against the door it was impossible to make out the words. She picked up her duster and flicked it over the dresser as Anne stumbled into her room. For one unguarded moment, she seemed frightened, until she spotted Frances. A sullen expression flitted over her face. 'Aren't you done yet?'

Frances curtsied. She hung her head. 'I'm sorry, miss. I could come back later to do the dusting.'

'No. I've got a headache. I need absolute quiet.'

'Yes, Miss.' Frances hurried away. She didn't believe in the headache, but she did believe that Anne wanted to be undisturbed in her room. But why? If only she could return and do a decent search of the room. She had concentrated on making the beds and looking for a damp coat or sweater. What if the cosh or sandbag or whatever weapon had been used was hidden in one of the rooms?

Aunt Mildred caught up with her as she approached the dead man's room. Jack must have giver her the key because she unlocked it and locked it again behind them.

Inside, they sat down together for a minute of silence. The pillow and eiderdown were untouched, the way Frances had left them, and a dressing-gown hung over the chair. An ashtray with five cigarette stubs and a bookmarked novel by Jules Verne sat on the bedside table next to the chair. and his slippers stood next to the dress shoes.

'Was he a heavy smoker?' Frances asked.

'Not as a habit, no.' Aunt Mildred bent over the stubs. 'All the same brand. No visitors, then.'

'He must have sat here and waited until it was time for his meeting.' Frances hugged herself. The poor man, reading and smoking to pass the hours, unaware that he would be going to his death.

'Shall I start with the clothes?' Frances asked. 'I

wouldn't be able to say which toiletries were his in the bathroom.'

'Tommy should know. Or, no, he wouldn't.' Aunt Mildred, normally unflappable, seemed at a loss.

'Who unpacked for him?'

'Bowman, so we could keep Onslow's work secret.' Aunt Mildred touched Frances's arm. 'I'm so glad you're all here to help us through this.'

To make sure they did not miss anything, Frances searched under the mattress and the sheet, before they put Onslow's suitcase on the bed. They patted down each garment before Frances folded it and put it away. Sadness welled up in her as she saw the evening shirts and the dinner jacket. Onslow had lacked Tommy's warmth and Jordan's charm, but he had been courteous, and most of all, alive. Even if he had stolen the blueprints, he did not deserve to end up lying dead in a garage in France.

They almost overlooked the notebook, because Onslow had cleverly hidden it inside the dust jacket of a slim book about engineering. The only clue that gave it away was the fact that the dust jacket was a couple of millimetres too wide and slipped a little.

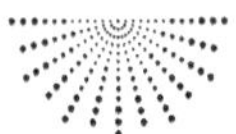

CHAPTER THIRTEEN

The notebook contained only half a dozen pages with notes in them. Frances stared at them from every angle she could think of, without making sense of them. Aunt Mildred was just as stumped.

Onslow, with his engineering background, had used a cipher, involving letters and symbols that might stand for numbers, or anything really, Frances thought. She pocketed the notebook. 'I hope Mr Fitzpatrick can make head and tail of this.'

Other than that, the only objects of interest were an unfinished letter to "Dearest Sophie", whom Frances took to be the sister. It read innocently enough. *'The party is in full swing, and the weather is clement enough to make one forget the dreariness at home. Maybe we should take a small house here ourselves next winter, you, and me, and Aunt to look after us. The only fly in the current ointment is the constant presence of the same kind of crowd that surrounds me at work. There is a forced artificiality to our gatherings, but I won't bother you with that. Our hostess has invited a new guest, whom I find most intriguing.'* Here, the writing broke off.

The second object was a photographic box camera. Despite its compact size, it was too big to fit in Frances's pockets.

'We could pack it away in the suitcase,' she said. 'But what if there is a film roll inside and it gets stolen?'

Aunt Mildred turned the leather-covered box camera in her hands. 'Do you know how to take out the film without damaging it?'

'I've seen Jack do it,' Frances said doubtfully, 'but this one is another brand.' She read the name. 'Agfa. I've never heard of it. What if it's different to Jack's Leica?'

'Then we must get him here. He'll have to come and carry down the suitcase.'

'That should work.' Frances had another idea. 'Did the others know Mr Onslow had a camera with him?'

Aunt Mildred mulled this over. 'I don't think so. Tommy has taken a few pictures of the girls by the pier with his old Brownie, because Lydia asked him to, but I don't recall Mr Onslow ever mentioning photography, or a camera.'

'Then maybe he didn't need to steal Uncle Sal's documents. He could just have taken their pictures.'

Aunt Mildred left Frances alone in the room. She

stripped the bed. A faint smell of Peter Onslow's pomade clung to the pillowcase, as a last reminder of his short existence.

Outside, a heavy vehicle drew up. Frances peeked out of the window. Two men in sombre black climbed out of an old ambulance and strode towards the garage. She turned her back to the window, no wanting to see them carry put the corpse.

Jack joined her a few minutes later. She flung herself into his arms as soon as he has closed the doors behind him. Tears ran down her nose.

'It's okay, my love,' he said. He produced a handkerchief.

'It's just, he was so young, and now he's dead.' They had solved murder cases before, but she had always been spared the sight of the dead body, or the weight of seeing a letter to a young girl at a boarding-school, who was now all alone in the world.

She blew her nose. 'Where are they taking him?'

'The local morgue. Fitzpatrick has arranged everything.'

'What if the doctor there says as well that it was an accident? If there is a doctor?'

'Fitzpatrick will take care of that. Hush-hush or not, he will not let a murder go unavenged. Now, show me that camera.'

He admired the compact design. 'Say what you want, but the Germans really are marvels when it comes to technical inventions.' He turned his back to her as he studied the camera design in the daylight flooding in through the window. 'There; all done.'

In his hand he held the film roll. 'What a pity I can't switch it for one of my film rolls. Wrong size.'

'Maybe you can find one in Nice,' she said. 'It would be easy to spread the good oil about this box camera.'

'Which might tempt our villain to take a closer geek at it.' He planted a kiss on her nose. 'Like I said, smartest girl I've ever met.' He snapped the suitcase with the camera inside shut and lifted it.

'Did Mr Bowman find a damp coat in the cloak room?' she asked.

'Too right he did.'

'And?'

'It was his own.'

Jack carried the suitcase downstairs. Frances had also handed him the cryptic notebook.

Aunt Mildred stood at the bottom of the stairs, wrapped in a plain brown coat, the closest she came to proper mourning clothes. 'Please bring the car around, Sullivan,' she said in a nice clear voice.

'Yes, Madam. Where do you want me to put the luggage?' Tiny head movements signalled that she needed to keep the suitcase around.

'Bowman,' she called out.

The butler appeared as if he'd been waiting for this cue, which he possibly had, Jack thought.

'Please lock the suitcase away, until I have spoken to the family,' Aunt Mildred demanded.

Jack screwed the distributor cap back into place. The only signs of the body's short stay in the garage were a few pine needles on the ground. He frowned as he shut the hood. There grew no pines along the marble staircase.

Aunt Mildred gracefully accepted his help to climb onto the passenger seat. 'I assume Mr Fitzpatrick is awaiting us.'

'Unless he is still at the morgue.' Jack hadn't dared waste too much time on the phone. The bike ride to the phone box took long enough, but Fitzpatrick luckily didn't need much explanation.

'This is a fine mess,' Aunt Mildred said. 'If only I hadn't agreed to this scheme.'

'He might have been murdered just the same, only in a different place.'

'Yes, but in that case, at least Tommy would be out of it.'

'Tommy? Only a fool would suspect him of any wrongdoing, and Fitzpatrick might be a bit pompous, but he's not an idiot.'

'There will still be a stain on my nephew's reputation.' Aunt Mildred wrung her fingers. 'There are no worse gossips than the British upper class.'

He thought about comforting her with a platitude, but she was too shrewd and too honest for that.

'Then we better give them something else to wag their tongues about,' he said.

With Jack and Aunt Mildred both gone, Frances appreciated the excuse Tinkerbell gave her for escaping the villa. The little dog frolicked about, his tail stub going a mile a minute as he sniffed grass and flower. An insolent magpie screamed at him, but in true aristocratic manner, Tink ignored it. Only seafowl could shake his good nature.

Frances avoided the area around the marble staircase. Instead, she threw Tink's ball further down, past the tennis courts, and towards the orangerie. She gazed back at the villa. Not a single person was in sight. Tink returned with his ball in his mouth. She took it from him and headed straight for the orangerie.

'This skulking around is trickier than I thought,' Uncle Sal said. He sat with a good view of the doors. The sun hit the glass, warming it up nicely. It was hard to believe it was winter.

Frances joined him. Tink gambolled about, happy to explore. 'I wish I had an excuse to go into town with you and Jack,' she said. 'But if Aunt Mildred needs anything, it would be strange for her to take me instead of Mrs Foster.'

'Have you found anything?' Uncle Sal tilted his face to the sun.

'He had a photographic camera,' she said. 'And a notebook with jumbled-up notes.'

Uncle Sal rubbed his nose, pondering.

'How did the guests react?' she asked.

'Lydia ran away from the table,' he said. 'She seemed genuinely upset. With her mother it's hard to tell under all that powder and rouge, but I'd say she had no idea. Neither had the other young lady, although she did not scarper.'

'But they came up together.' Tink rubbed against Frances's ankle. She rubbed his back. 'Or at the most half a minute apart. If Lydia left the breakfast table long before the others, where has she been?'

'The bathroom?'

'Not the one on the guest floor, or I would have heard her.' She made a mental note to inform Mr Bowman. If only they could all meet at least once a day to compare information, their life would be a lot easier. 'What about the gentlemen?'

'They went all British and stiff upper lip. Jordan and Onslow had some words last night, but nothing serious, or he wouldn't have admitted it. Bassington-Whyte appeared a trifle out of sorts although he had less to drink than usual. With Morris it's hard to guess anything. Tommy should be able to shed a little light on him. If only we could be sure why Onslow was murdered.'

'A falling out among thieves?' Frances suggested. 'Or he wanted too much money for your blueprints, and the murderer thought he could put his hands on them without Onslow?'

'But how did he expect to do that if the papers are still in my possession? Unless he took pictures, and the murderer stole them.'

'Then the film roll Jack found has to be a new one.' Frances jumped up. Tink saw that as a sign to make a play for his ball. 'Come on, Tinkerbell.' She flung the ball out of the door and back towards the villa. Duty, and a chat with Mr Bowman, called.

'Shall I have some tea sent down for you?' she asked Uncle Sal. That would probably be Mr Bowman's duty, which meant an opportunity for him to chat with Uncle Sal.

'I'd better go up too,' he said. 'Another pair of eyes to watch what's going on.'

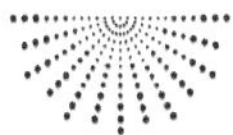

'I wish we had more observers in the house.' Fitzpatrick lit another cigarette from the stub of the first one, before he offered Jack and Aunt Mildred his case. That was the only outward sign that he was shaken.

His trip to the morgue had ended soon after the two had arrived. Colette had taken them up to his room. She had dropped her frivolous mask from the night at the Palais de Jetee completely. A neat suit and a stenographer's pad reminded Jack of her double role.

'Are you going to send someone else down to the villa?' Aunt Mildred asked. 'Under different circumstances I could invite your niece.'

'No.' Fitzpatrick took a deep drag. 'I don't want to tip our hand. I'm afraid our set-up remains unchanged.'

'Have you seen the bruise on the body?' Jack knocked the ash off his cigarette.

'You're a good observer. The doctor – one we've worked with before in an official capacity, not the one who came out to the villa – confirmed that Onslow was knocked unconscious, before he had his neck broken. The fact that there was barely a trickle of blood from a huge gash is additional proof, and there were marks on his collar that corresponded with faint marks on his skin, from a hand.'

Colette swallowed hard. Aunt Mildred touched her arm in a gesture of comfort. 'It is not a pleasant thought.'

'It's a ghastly picture.' The young woman shivered.

'The storm made the accident plausible enough,' Jack said. 'I wouldn't be too hard on Dr Durand. He had no reason to be suspicious.'

'Luckily.' Fitzpatrick stubbed out his cigarette and steepled his hands under his chin. 'Having all and sundry know we are dealing with a murder is the last thing we want.'

A knock on the door interrupted them. Colette went to open and returned with a small parcel. 'Your film rolls.'

Jack held out his hands. They had telephoned ahead, to warn Fitzpatrick, or rather Colette, what they needed. The original roll was already in a dark room with an unspecified government agent. Jack wondered how many men the British government had at their disposal here in the South of France, but they would likely have arrangements to help each other on an official or rather unofficial level.

Another two or three hours, and they should see results. If the film roll was unused, they would have known by now. Which meant, Onslow had left them at least one photograph. As soon as they returned, Jack intended to replace the film roll and keep the other one, in case they needed it as additional bait.

Colette puzzled over the notebook. She faithfully copied every letter and symbol which would be passed on to an encryption specialist.

'Can I have a copy?' Jack felt something stirring at the back of his mind, the longer he perused Colette's scribbles.

Fitzpatrick sat silent for a moment. 'I can't see why not, if you are sure it is possible to keep it safe,' he said. 'Onslow took that notebook along for a reason, and I don't want whatever he wrote to fall into the wrong hands.'

The phone rang. Fitzpatrick lifted the receiver. 'Yes? --- Put him through.' He mouthed, "Bowman", before he listened again. He held the receiver two inches from his ear, so they could hear the butler.

'Is this the Palais de Jetee?'

They shared a puzzled look.

'Yes, that is correct.' Fitzpatrick gave the others a tiny shrug as he played along.

'It is far-fetched, but the night before New Year's, we

had a large party attending your establishment. The Right Honourable Mrs Clifton and guests.'

'Yes?'

'It appears one of our visitors has lost a bracelet, platinum, with baguette-cut diamonds and round-cut sapphires. It is extremely valuable.'

Aunt Mildred's hand flew to her mouth. Jack waved the statement off.

'Have the police been informed?' Fitzpatrick asked.

'Not yet. The lady in question did not want to make a fuss, when she might have simply lost it at your establishment.'

'I shall make the necessary enquiries. Thank you very much. Where can we reach you?'

'At *Les Palms*.' Bowman added the phone number and rang off.

'A lost bracelet, and you didn't mention it?' Fitzpatrick lit another cigarette.

'Because it's not true,' Jack said. 'I've never clapped eyes on that piece of jewellery, but if you owned a piece like that and lost it, would you wait for three days until you mentioned it?'

'Dorothy Bassington-Whyte and her daughter do own a few lovely jewels,' Aunt Mildred said. 'It is possible that Lydia wore that bracelet to the party. Geraldine, the maid who helped her, would know.'

'Geraldine was the one who spotted that most of your friends' jewellery was paste,' Jack reminded her.

'But what if this bracelet was the real thing, and Onslow took it? If he betrayed his own country by stealing blueprints sensitive to our defence, and selling them, why not add another theft?' Colette asked.

'In that case he might have been killed for the bracelet.' Aunt Mildred's voice sounded thin, and for the first time, old.

CHAPTER FIFTEEN

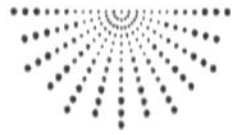

The same idea had struck Frances and Mr Bowman.

Frances had returned to the villa, to find Geraldine in tears. 'I didn't do anything,' she wailed. Frances thanked their lucky stars that the butler's pantry, where the maid cried up a storm, was well out of earshot.

Mr Bowman towered over Geraldine who grasped Frances's hands as if they alone could save her.

'What's going on?' Frances's conscience made itself unpleasantly felt. What if anybody had noticed the missing notebook or film and they suspected poor Geraldine?

'It's the bracelet. Miss Lydia's.' Hiccup made it hard to understand the words. 'It should be in her jewellery box and it isn't.'

'How can you possibly be sure?' Frances asked.

Geraldine's hiccup stopped at the stupid question, only to come back at double the intensity.

Bowman made her let go of Frances and gave her a tot of brandy, which helped calm her down. 'Lady Bassington-Whyte told me to fetch any jet jewellery I could find, because the house is in mourning. Miss Bassington-Whyte was in the bath, so I went into her room. The bracelet isn't there, and I haven't seen it since the night before New Year's eve. She didn't wear it for that party, because she took her rubies. But the night before, she had on her blue evening frock that looks ever so lovely with the bracelet.'

'Maybe she loaned it to her friend or her mother,' Frances said. 'Did she wear it when you helped her undress that night?'

Geraldine's brows furrowed in an effort to remember. 'She might have. She always took off her earrings herself.'

'But a bracelet usually has a difficult clasp,' Mr Bowman said.

The maid sniffed. 'She always tried herself. I think she didn't want me to get a close peek because most of the gems were as fake as my uncle's teeth.'

Frances giggled at the comparison.

'Did Miss Bassington-Whyte accuse you of any wrongdoing?' The butler gave Geraldine a stern look.

'No. She told me to leave her alone because she needed rest. I just thought I'd tell you myself.' Geraldine wiped her nose with her sleeve before she blushed at her common behaviour.

'You did the right thing. Just leave everything to me.' Mr Bowman dismissed Geraldine.

'You go get a bit of rest,' Frances said to the maid. 'I'll bring you a nice cup of tea.'

'Ta ever so much.' Much comforted, Geraldine took herself off.

Mrs Foster sat in the kitchen, chatting with the cook, and Frances simply told them that Geraldine was unwell, and the butler had instructed her to have a lie down.

'Poor thing,' Mrs Foster said, before she added ominously, 'I only hope that it's nothing she comes to regret.' Madame Petit nodded in sympathy and added two biscuits to the tea tray.

'Why?' Frances asked. 'What's wrong?'

'I'm not one to gossip, but she wouldn't be the first one to have her head turned over a little flattery and promises.'

Frances took a wild guess. 'I thought I'd heard Geraldine whisper with a man once.'

'Mr Bassington-Whyte?' Mrs Foster shot her a sharp glance.

'I couldn't say. I better run and bring her the tea before it gets cold.'

Frances knocked on Geraldine's door. The maid's hands clutched the blanket which she had pulled up to her chin. She looked a little like a frightened child, but also slightly pleased with herself.

Her eyes went round as she spotted the biscuits. 'They're the posh ones, from the tin reserved for madam.'

'Cook thought you could do with a treat.' A sharp intake of breath told Frances that she had said the wrong thing. 'I only told her and Mrs Foster that you are unwell.' She added a lump of sugar to the tea and stirred it for Geraldine who sat up against the pillow.

'Must be nice for fancy people to have a bit of a lie-down whenever they feel like it,' Geraldine said. 'It's ever so nice when you're all shook, like.'

'Why do you think Miss Bassington-Whyte kept silent about the bracelet?'

A drop of tea spilt onto the blanket as Geraldine set her cup down on her lap. 'Do you think she knows who took it? Or maybe she sold it.'

'When could she have done that? And you said, it's paste.'

'That one might not have been. But her long diamond earrings are, and her pearls.'

'How can you tell?'

'My dad used to work for a pawnbroker. I used to go after school and do the sweeping and such, and the owner taught me. With pearls, you can tell when you rub them. If they're all smooth, they're fake. And if you hold them to the skin, real pearls are cold for a tick, and then they get all nice and warm.'

'You should be working for a jeweller,' Frances said with genuine admiration. She sat down on the bed.

'Or wear precious things.' Geraldine smiled to herself.

'Then you have to keep your fingers crossed that your beau becomes the most successful baker in all of England or hope for an inheritance.'

'Hah. There are other ways.'

'There are?'

Geraldine preened. 'You wouldn't know about real gentlefolk, in Australia, but sometimes when you do a favour to the right person, they're proper grateful.' She rubbed thumb and index finger together,

'Oooh,' Frances said in an encouraging tone.

'Mind you, he never said as much.'

So, there was a "he" involved.

'As long as they don't take any liberties,' Frances said. 'I've heard awful things.'

Geraldine sipped her tea and nibbled a biscuit, careful to avoid crumbs. 'Mr Bassington-Whyte would never do that, and anyway, my mum brought me up decent, she did.'

'Then what did Mr Bassington-Whyte want from you?'

'Just a favour.' Geraldine's face took on a sly expression.

Frances decided not to push the matter any further. 'I should run,' she said.

Geraldine closed her eyes. 'Tell Mr Bowman I'll try to be down for lunch.'

'Well done,' Mr Bowman said softly as Frances recounted her conversation with the maid.

'What do we do next?' She opened the cutlery drawer, to lay the table for the staff. She would do the dining room next.

'I thought it best to pass on the information about the bracelet without delay,' he said. 'I hope when madam comes back, that she will be able to shed a little more light on the situation.'

'It's all a bit much, isn't it?' Frances cocked her ears for any sounds, although it would have been physically impossible for anyone to earwig on their chat, so sturdy were the walls and the door of the butler's pantry. 'Stolen documents, a dead man, and missing jewels.'

'These things have to be related,' Mr Bowman agreed. 'If not, we're in even deeper trouble.'

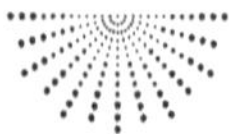

*A*unt Mildred insisted on a decent lunch for them all while they waited for the photographs. Room service left a lot to be desired, but it eliminated the risk of being seen together in public.

The bouillabaisse followed by steak frites made up for the sullen waiter, but Jack had a hard time stopping himself staring at the door impatiently. This was all taking too long. What if the laboratory assistant botched up the development process? And what if the folks back at the villa became suspicious because the hostess had disappeared for hours just after one of her own guests had died?

The phone rang again. Fitzpatrick put down his knife and fork and gulped down his bite of steak to answer. 'Yes? – Thank you.'

He addressed Colette. 'There's a courier waiting at the

reception, with a large envelope. Can you please pick it up? I'd rather no-one outside our little group is aware we're working together.'

Colette took a hat from the wardrobe. She pulled it deep into her face, making her completely unrecognisable as the flirtatious young lady they had met at the Palais de Jetees.

'Let us hope Onslow has left us a decent trail to follow.' Fitzpatrick picked up knife and fork again. 'If we can't figure out why he died soon, all our suspects will go home, and we're beaten.'

'How much longer do we have?'

'The railway tickets are booked for Thursday morning.'

'Less than five days.' Jack pushed away his empty plate.

'Yes.'

The envelope that Colette brought up had a promising bulk. Fitzgerald slit it open and emptied the contents on the desk. The technician had done his best and delivered five individual pictures, each in different sizes or changes in exposure.

They stared at them. Instead of the blueprints in Uncle Sal's possession, Onslow had chosen to photograph the fake letters that accompanied them.

'I don't understand,' Aunt Mildred said. 'Of what use are these letters?'

'They have none.' Fitzpatrick blew out his breath. 'So, why did he take them?'

'Unless he thought they would lead him to whoever Uncle Sal's prospective buyers were.'

'Why, if he had his own contacts? Wouldn't these people, if they existed, be suspicious if anyone else but Uncle Sal approached them?' Jack spoke as much to himself as to the others. That niggling idea at the back of his mind came into the foreground. He reached for Onslow's cipher.

The notes covered the lines without indentations or punctuation, but each was separated by two symbols, eight letters and another four symbols.

'I think he kept a diary,' Jack said slowly. 'If I'm right, these lines are the dates. In which case we already have the 1, the 9, and the 3, followed by another 1, for 1931.'

He checked. The two symbols he took to be the 1 were identical. 'That means, we also have the letters E, M, B, and R. It's unlikely that these notes were written earlier than December or November, at a push.'

'In which case our cryptographers have a good chance of breaking the cipher without much trouble.' Fitzpatrick clapped Jack on the back.

'It's probably a simple substitution code,' Jack said. 'Either that, or a book code, in which case we need to check all the books he had with him.'

'How does a substitution code work?' Aunt Mildred asked. 'And why would he write things down?'

'Maybe he kept them as a private diary, or to make notes about progress with negotiations. He'd write down the alphabet and number from 0 to 9 and give them all new letters or numbers. That can be done by just shifting their position, for example an a becomes a b, a b becomes a c,' Fitzpatrick said. He shrugged as he saw his niece's impressed look. 'I did my stint of intelligence work during the war. One remembers things.'

'He was a trained engineer. It's much likelier that he made up his own version and either memorised it or created a template of sorts,' Jack said. 'We have to go through his belongings again.'

Aunt Mildred took the parcel with black armbands and black gloves they had used as an excuse. 'We have no time to lose, especially if I want to grill Dorothy and Lydia about the bracelet.'

'I'll wait for your answers,' Fitzpatrick said.

'It might be night-time. I'll have to use the phone box again,' Jack warned him.

'That doesn't matter. Just promise me you will be careful, all of you. Once a man has committed one murder, he has nothing to lose. Even if he believes he fooled us.'

CHAPTER SEVENTEEN

*A*unt Mildred swept into the drawing room where the ladies took their tea. Only Lydia looked as if she had cried, but the other two had at least the good grace to be in a sombre mood.

'I'm so sorry I took me so long to make these purchases,' Aunt Mildred said, and put down the parcel.

Fresh tears welled up in Lydia's eyes, but that might well be the result of the eyelash darkener the young woman used in copious amounts. Aunt Mildred had tried it once, and it had made her eyes water for hours.

Anne put her cup down. 'Please excuse me.'

Interesting, Aunt Mildred thought. Either she wanted to give them space or she disliked the display of Lydia's tears.

'What a terrible, terrible day,' she said. 'I've heard we had more unpleasantness while I was out.'

Lydia's mother dropped the handkerchief she held in her hand.

Her daughter clutched her temples. 'My headache is returning,'

Aunt Mildred rang the bell for Bowman.

'Yes. Madam?'

'Please fetch the aspirin,' she said. 'And tell cook to prepare a dinner tray for Miss Bassington-Whyte, to be brought to her room tonight.'

'Very well.'

Lydia opened her mouth. Aunt Mildred shushed her. 'You will soon feel better,' she said. She waited until Bowman returned and the patient had taken two pills with water, before she tackled her. 'I've been told that you've lost a valuable piece of jewellery.'

Lydia's gaze searched her mother's. Lady Bassington-Whyte moistened her dry lips. 'We didn't want to make a fuss. It is probably somewhere in Lydia's room. She can be a little careless, as I've reminded her for years.'

'Surely the maid would have found it? Or are my staff neglecting their duties?'

'No. not at all. Good god, the very idea never entered my mind.'

'When did you miss the bracelet?' Aunt Mildred's face showed nothing but tender sympathy.

'Sometime after the evening at the Palais de Jetees.' Lydia's voice grew quieter and quieter.

'Why didn't you say anything? The police would have had a much easier job straight away.'

'The police?' Lydia shrieked. ''Why, there is certainly no need for that. The stupid bracelet is insured anyway.'

'I am afraid it is unavoidable. There will have to be an investigation unless the Palais manager can locate your jewels today. I have taken the liberty to inform them,' Bowman said. 'If you can't say for certain where the item went missing, it is important to clear the staff from any suspicion that might otherwise fall upon them.'

'An investigation?' Crimson circles appeared on Lady Bassington-Whyte's cheek, directly under her artificial rouge.

'Maybe it fell off in the car, on our way home.' Lydia twisted her fingers. 'Mother and I will go and search.'

'There's no need, Miss Lydia. Sullivan and I will take care of it.' Bowman slipped out of the door and noiselessly closed it behind him.

They found Tommy hanging about outside the garage, playing with Tink. 'Nobody even tried to come close to Uncle Sal's room while you were gone,' he said quietly. Louder he said, 'A treasure hunt, eh? Jolly good.'

Jack unlocked the garage and closed it up behind them.

Tommy rubbed his hands in expectation. 'Open her up, Jack, and let's search the car.'

'I wouldn't bet on discovering the bracelet.'

'Of course not.' Tink woofed as if he wanted to show he agreed with his master. 'But I bet there will be odds and ends lying around, after all your driving us around. If we don't come back with at least a handkerchief to show, it is hard to sell this as a proper job.'

Jack grinned. It was easy to forget how smart Tommy really was under that inoffensive facade. He must have been bored too, with not much more to contribute than keeping an eye on the other men.

'Where are your friends now?' Jack asked.

'Jordan and Morris are playing at billiards again, and Bassington-Whyte is hogging the bathroom. He takes forever these days with his grooming. It would have appeared odd for me to hang around.'

Tommy slid his hand across the backseat and peered on the floor. 'What did I tell you?' He held up an enamelled powder compact. 'Anne's, if I'm not mistaken.'

'Wouldn't she have noticed the loss?'

Puzzled, Tommy crinkled his nose. 'I'd say so. Those girls constantly freshen up their faces.'

'Maybe she has another one, for the day, and keeps this in her evening purse.' Mr Bowman finished his search of the front. 'Maybe your aunt can clear that up.'

They settled down, to bring Tommy up to speed. He goggled at the mention of the photographs, and the notebook. 'That's clever, but then Onslow always struck me as having a good head on his shoulders. You saw him at the gambling table. Careful bets, no more than two drinks, and ready to cut his losses without thinking twice.'

'Very different from Bassington-Whyte,' Jack said.

'Yes, although the funny thing is, he used to be a lot more like Onslow, at least whenever I ran into him at one of his clubs.'

'Really? When did that change?'

'Maybe six month ago?'

'When did Fitzpatrick say the old lady drained their resources?' Jack asked the butler.

Bowman checked his notebook. 'By the end of 1930. When the market crashed, she found it impossible to adjust to much reduced circumstances. It says here, she hired a psychic, to guide her to the treasure purportedly hidden by her husband's grandfather.'

'A hidden treasure? Don't tell me the old boy used to be a pirate.' Tommy chuckled.

'Almost. He made his fortune trading opium.'

'And hid the proceeds rather than pass them on?'

'That's what Lady Bassington-Whyte believed. She paid her phony spiritualist a couple of thousand, for nothing.' Bowman put his notebook away.

'What a sap that woman is,' Tommy said. 'Poor bastard, he probably stumbled upon the empty coffers when people started knocking on the door.'

'Which gives him an excellent motive to muscle in on

Onslow's game. The family needs a lot of money to be sitting pretty again,' Jack said.

'The same goes for his sister, and the mother. I know it's hard to believe that a woman would be involved in a murder, but it's possible that Lydia lured Onslow outside, and her brother did the rest,' Bowman said.

'That part is plausible,' Jack agreed, although Tommy appeared doubtful. 'But would he honestly think she'd meet him in such beastly weather?'

'That depends on why they arranged the rendezvous.' Tommy ruffled his hair. 'I thought for a while she was a bit goofy on him, but maybe that was just a front. Maybe she found out about his little trip to Uncle Sal's room and demanded money.'

'Because whatever she did with the bracelet didn't bring in enough. That's an idea.' The butler checked his watch. 'I should return to my official duties.'

Tommy nodded. 'Tink? Come here, boy.' The corgi wagged his tail stub but stayed in the corner where the body had lain.

Tommy ambled over, to see the dog sniff the ground.

'What is it?'

He waved Jack over. 'I think Tink found something.' He picked up a pine needle.

'They were clinging to Onslow's body. I have no idea how they got there.'

'Which part of the body?'

Jack pondered this. 'The leg, just where the body fell onto the broken palm fronds.'

'Far away from the pine trees.'

'Too right.'

'Mr Bowman.' Tommy signalled the butler to join them. 'Do we have the fronds?'

Although he really couldn't tell why, Jack had kept them in a box under the workbench. He touched the damaged parts. 'They fit with the theory that he caught his heel on them and tumbled down the stairs.'

'But then his body wouldn't have landed on them.'

'It didn't. These were two steps further up. He fell onto these.' Jack showed the other two another frond with two damaged leaves.

'And the pine needles?' A grin from ear to ear spread over Tommy's face.

'I'd say around the same location.'

'Would you lie down for a moment?'

Jack refrained from asking why. He spread a canvas tarpaulin on the ground and arranged himself the way Onslow had lain, with arms stretched out in front of him and one leg at an angle.

'Which trouser leg did the needles cling to?'

'The left one.'

Tommy gently nudged his foot under Jack's leg and lifted it so he could push the palm frond underneath. Then he pulled his foot out again.

'That's all,' he said.

Jack rose.

'Leave the tarpaulin for a moment.' Bowman squatted. 'Pine needles.'

'I got some stuck to the sole of my shoe,' Tommy said. 'A few days ago, before Frances replaced the old maid, I trod them all over the orangerie. They must have come off when the murderer dug his heel into the palm frond.'

'Which means, with any luck there will still be a few left on his soles.'

'It's at least an idea. Excellent thinking.' Bowman nodded to himself. 'That means, when the guests are at dinner, we shall inspect everyone's shoes.'

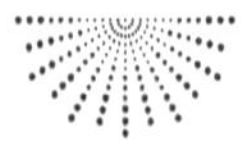

Tommy marched whistling to the drawing room. Before he entered, he arranged his face in an affable, yet blank expression. 'Hullo, there,' he cried out.

'Have you found the jewellery?' Aunt Mildred sat next to Lady Bassington-Whyte who took solace in a snifter of brandy. Lydia had gone, but in her place, Anne perched on the edge of a chair. Her stiff posture contradicted the pretend indifference with which she leafed through a well-thumbed novel by Elizabeth von Arnim.

'No bracelet, I'm afraid. But we did unearth other treasure.' Lady Bassington-Whyte's head shot up, and Anne lowered her novel.

With a flourish, Tommy produced the powder compact. 'I say, it's incredible the things you can lose in those car seats. Makes you wonder what the taxi drivers find, eh.'

'That's mine, thank you.' Anne rewarded him with a pained smile.

'It's a pretty thing. I thought you would have missed it.'

She did not answer.

'Right-ho,' he said, to fill the silence.

'Be a dear and take the black armbands around,' Aunt Mildred said.

He dropped his carefree mask and adopted a solemn one. 'Certainly.'

Tommy peeked into the games room.

'There you are, Clifton.' Jordan cocked his head towards the cue rack. 'Fancy a quick round?'

'I'm not done yet,' Morris said as he took aim at a ball. 'Even your infernal luck must give out.'

'It's my clear head and pure heart that do it.'

As if to prove Jordan's words, his opponent missed and watched helplessly as Jordan cleared the table.

Tommy put the box with the armbands onto the drinks table.

'Gosh,' Morris said. 'These miserable things really bring it home, don't they? I thought we'd be done with them when the war ended.'

'Does your aunt expect us to wear them in the house?' Jordan wound an armband around his sleeve.

'No, I think it's just when we go out, isn't it?' Tommy

helped himself to a drink, feeling almost as foolish as he made out to be. 'Would be terribly bad form otherwise.'

'Or at the funeral?' Now Jordan poured a drink for himself and for Morris. 'It will probably have to be held here unless the aunt has claimed the body.'

'I didn't think of that.' Tommy wondered if Fitzpatrick had.

'No. Bloody unpleasant, all of this. At least back home one could ring up the funeral home and make arrangements.' Jordan rolled his cue stick across the table. 'Of all the things to happen, to break your neck like this…'

Morris put his hand over his stomach. Maybe he really was sensitive. Or a good actor. Tommy asked him, 'You two were close, weren't you?'

'As close as with anyone in the department. He was a bit of an odd fish, very brainy, and yet he was constantly tinkering with something mechanical, like one of the workmen.'

'I thought you had some engineering knowledge as well.' Jordan put the cue away. He sat down and crossed his ankles. With relief, Tommy noticed that both men wore dress shoes, with smooth soles. Definitely not the footwear to go out in on a rainy night.

'Purely theoretical,' Morris said. 'I can read a circuit plan as well as the next man but ask me to construct anything more difficult than a paper plane, and I'm out.'

'Still better than me.' Jordan's teeth gleamed as he

broke into a genuine smile. 'I don't have the hand for anything fiddly.'

'Ridiculous,' Morris said. 'I've seen you, fixing the mechanism in that old pocket watch of yours.'

'Only because I grew up doing that. The stupid thing spends more time broken than running correctly.' With infinite care, Jordan stroked his vintage pocket watch.

'How old is it?' Tommy asked. For someone as modern and proud of it as Jordan, to keep fiddling with an antique at all appeared out of the ordinary.

'Almost a hundred years old. A gift from Queen Victoria to my great-great-grandfather.'

'Onslow would have been able to fix it once and for all,' Morris said. 'I can't believe he's gone.'

The first gong rang out, a signal that they had half an hour left to change for dinner.

Tommy went over the conversation again in his head as he dashed to his suite. Morris would be the perfect candidate to figure out that Uncle Sal's blueprints might be worth a lot of money to the right seller. He had also been the one who filed away the stolen documents in the wrong place, thus making sure that Onslow took the originals along to France. What if that had not been an accident, but planned, and the two had worked together?

And what about his friend Jordan? He possessed stronger nerves than Morris displayed, and he also had an eye for detail and patience, or he would have given up repairing the watch years ago.

Did that mean they could cross off Bassington-Whyte, who certainly had neither a great head for detail, or he'd be a better card player, nor mechanical abilities, as far as Tommy could tell? But then, to sell stolen documents demanded none of these skills, only the right contacts. If that was why Onslow had been murdered.

It all came down to this one big 'if', he thought as he adjusted his tie. The second gong rang. Five minutes until dinner, and the shoe inspection.

Frances longed to be alone with Jack just for a few minutes. Instead, she had to pretend to be indifferent to him, while a visibly recovered Geraldine recounted again the fright the missing bracelet had given her.

Finally, Mrs Foster had enough. She said, 'If Mr Bowman said you have nothing to worry about, then you have nothing to worry about. You would do well to think about how to help madam, when there's a death in the house, instead of letting Frances do your work on top of her own.'

'It was fine,' Frances said.

'Mr Bowman said as I should have a bit of lie-down,' Geraldine pouted.

'I did indeed, and I am glad to see it helped. You will please do the dishes tonight, so Madame Petit can have the night off. After all, she found the body, which must have been quite a shock.'

The cook gave a shudder. 'I will never forget it. Le pauvre jeune homme.'

'You were very brave,' Frances said.

'People of our generation were brought up to do our duty,' Mrs Foster said. 'We never shied away from it, no matter the circumstances. I'm sure Mr Sullivan, as a former soldier, will understand.'

Cook nodded fervently.

Geraldine's lip wobbled.

'And Geraldine has been very brave as well,' Mr Bowman saved the situation. 'She made the right decision by coming to me.'

With a trembling hand, Geraldine fluffed up her hair. 'It was ever so hard to think of what to do, with Madam gone.'

The butler gave her another approving nod. 'And now I need both you and Mrs Foster to serve dinner in the dining room.'

'Us?' Foster stared at him in surprise.

'I'm afraid there are other, unpleasant, tasks to do, and Frances and Sullivan will both have to assist me.'

'But what –'

A headshake from Mrs Foster stopped Geraldine.

'I still can't believe Mr Onslow is dead.' Frances finished her meal. 'He had lovely manners, didn't he?'

'He did, and he never rang for anything or expected me to clean his clothes in a jiffy.'

'Did he have a fiancée?' Frances asked.

'I don't think so. There were no pictures in his room. But I think Miss Lydia must have been sweet on him, the way she's carrying on. This morning she ran out of the dining room and locked herself in the bathroom for ages, and she didn't turn on the tap.'

'A lady has her bath before breakfast, not after,' Mrs Foster said. 'And that is enough gossip.'

Bowman left the room, to strike the second dinner gong.

'Blow your nose, and put your cap on straight, Geraldine,' Foster said. 'Don't forget to keep your eyes down, and don't talk unless you're spoken to when we serve dinner.'

Frances waited until all the guests had come down, except for the poorly Lydia.

She whisked up to the guest floor and sneaked into Mr Morris's room. She took the first shoe, a stout walking boot, out of the wardrobe and peered at it closely. Nothing.

She replaced it and took the second one. This, too, showed no traces of pine needles, or the tiniest sign of having been wet and not brushed in the morning. Peter Onslow's death had seen to that. Normally, Frances would have collected any footwear left outside a door and taken it down for cleaning, but after the first shock, she had been too busy with other things.

If she remembered correctly, there also had been no shoes waiting to be brushed and polished. That would be due to the weather, she thought. Only a fool would have drawn attention to himself by putting out wet footwear.

Mr Morris's rubber-soled tennis shoes also passed her inspection, as did his wingtip shoes. She put them back and left the room.

'Frances?' Geraldine stared at her. In her hand she held an empty dinner tray. 'What are you doing?'

Frances's mind whirred. An excuse, quick. What could she have done in a gentlemen's room? 'Mr Bowman sent me to close the window. He heard it rattle.' She pulled a face. 'If he'd told me you would come up here as well, I would have asked you.'

'Dinner for Miss Lydia. Not that she'd say thank you.' Geraldine shrugged it off. 'What else are you doing for Mr Bowman?' Was it curiosity that made her question Frances's movements, or something else?

'Scrubbing,' she said. 'I'm just glad Mr Onslow didn't die in that room.'

Geraldine gulped. 'Better you than me.' She hurried to the servants' staircase.

That was a close shave. Frances tiptoed into Bassington-Whyte's room. Hopefully, the food would distract his sister, in the unlikely case that Frances made so much noise Lydia could hear it.

His shoes too proved to be free of pine needles or water stains, and so did Mr Jordan's. Frances even checked Anne's and Lady Bassington-Whyte's shoes.

Both owned heavy walking shoes, with ridged soles, and although Lady Bassington-Whyte's shoes had a damp spot on the top cap, she could not find anything else.

She trudged downstairs with a heavy heart, only to have Mr Bowman beckoning her. 'Quick,' he said,' did you find anything?'

'It appears as if Lady Bassington-Whyte was out in the rain, but that's all. Do we have any idea when it stopped?'

'Around two in the morning. If you help Jack with the suitcase again, I'll arrange –'

He stopped mid-sentence as Jack appeared. He gave Frances a swift hug. 'Someone's a very smart cove,' he said as he produced a handkerchief, with two pine needles inside.

Mr Bowman ushered them both into the butler's pantry. 'Where did you find them?'

'On a pair of galoshes. Size nine.'

Frances groaned, and Mr Bowman's shoulders sagged a little. 'They came with the house and are commonly shared.'

'A pair of galoshes everyone can take, your own overcoat to keep him dry – I told you he's a clever one. I take any bet his own feet are smaller than a nine. But we'll get him yet.' Jack chuckled.

'I don't see how the galoshes can help,' the butler said.

'No? The question is, why did he end up with pine needles on his soles, and a damp coat?'

'Because he went down to the tennis court, or close by.' Frances glanced at Jack for confirmation.

'And why would he do that?'

'To fetch the cosh or to hide it.' Bowman's shoulders straightened again. 'It's too late to search the area, but I think you're right.'

'This also means, our man thinks on his feet.'

'Why?' The butler frowned.

'Of course,' Frances said. 'If he had prepared in advance, he would have had a weapon handy that he could get rid of in the house, and that didn't demand he go out in the night. Something like cook's rolling-pin.'

Jack squeezed her hand as he beamed at her. 'And now for the suitcase again. I think it's a good idea to take it to my room and search it there.'

'But what if we need to plant the film roll?'

'The camera is valuable,' Jack said. 'Mr Bowman would be bad at his job if he didn't box it properly.'

Jack carried the luggage, while Frances and Mr Bowman brought up the rear and made sure they were unseen. The dining room had a set of French doors, but like the ones in the games room, they opened towards the garden and the marble staircase.

Frances grimaced. The silvery moonlight competed with the glow from Mr Bowman's torch. After last night's rain, the air had kept its sweet perfume. The whole setting was made for a romantic evening, with just herself and Jack strolling hand in hand, or dancing and kissing under the star-spangled sky.

Instead, they spent their waking hours masquerading as servants, secretly sleuthing.

The gravel behind her back crunched. She spun around as a small creature sat down in front of her, lolling his tongue. 'Tink.' She picked him up.

'There you are, you little scamp.' Tommy came running. He took the dog from Frances and muttered, 'You're wanted, Bowman. A phone call.'

The butler turned on his heel.

Tommy said, 'Uncle Sal told me to inform you that he and I won't be kept out of the action again, so whatever it is you're doing, wait until we can join you.'

'If you insist. I can do without rifling through another man's clothes.'

'No, if that's what's happening, you're welcome to do it.' Tommy winked at Frances. 'We're perfectly happy just watching.'

'In that case do you mind if I stow away the suitcase in your suite?' Jack asked. 'Uncle Sal can invite himself for a drink and a chat from man to man, and you should be able to come up with an excuse for me to tag along.'

'And what about me? I have no excuse.' Frances pushed out her bottom lip.

'Aunt Mildred can summon you while Foster runs her

bath, if you're quiet as a mouse. There's a connecting door between our dressing-rooms.' Tommy eyed the suitcase.

'Good-oh.' Frances cheered up. How lovely to have a proper meeting with her co-sleuths again.

'I have to dash,' Tommy said. 'You take care of Tink, which will make it only natural for you to come up to our rooms.' He handed Frances the little dog and its leash.

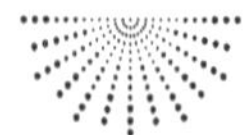

ncle Sal hid in the library behind his *Corriere della Sera*. The young men had decided to sit in the room as well, listening to the wireless and smoking. The ladies had retired already. A death in their midst had thrown a damper over everything.

'I think I'll go for a walk,' Morris said.

'Where to? There's nowhere to go, and we don't want another accident in the dark, do we?' Jordan reached for the whisky decanter.

'I might tag along.' Bassington-Whyte loosened his collar with two fingers. 'Still only eleven.'

With a huge yawn, Tommy rose. 'I don't know about you, but I could do with an early night. And I should see if Aunt Mildred's alright. She tries to keep up a brave face, but it's all been dashed hard on her.'

'Va bene,' Uncle Sal said. 'I too shall come and see

how our hostess is doing, and then you and I can have a chat about my newspaper.'

Without waiting for a response, he limped off. Tommy followed him with an apologetic shrug to the rest of the group.

That left only Bowman to keep guard, but because Jack had the Chevrolet's distributor cap safely hidden away, there would be no midnight flight.

'I'm sorry it took so long.' Tommy pecked his aunt on her cheek. 'It's all very cloak and dagger, with so many people skulking around.'

'As long as you're here.' She locked the door behind her. 'At least we will be undisturbed.'

'What about your maid?' Uncle Sal asked.

'I've sent her to bed.' Aunt Mildred opened the door to her dressing room. 'You can come out now,' she said to Jack and Frances, who shared an upholstered stool with Tinkerbell.

'Or we could join you,' Uncle Sal said. 'Some people have big ears.'

Tommy arranged enough seating for everyone in the dressing room. With five people inside she trusted, it gave Frances a snug and cosy feeling. After all the deception and lies of the last days, everything was right again for a short while.

She leant against Jack's shoulder, and he held her tight.

'Who was the phone call for Bowman from?' he asked. 'Anything Fitzpatrick should be told?'

'The manager of the Palais de Jetees confirmed that there was no bracelet found on the premises. My superior had called them pretending to be me. We can't afford to slip up anywhere on this case.'

'Lydia could still insist that a staff member might have taken it,' Frances said.

'She won't. She's already rattled.' Aunt Mildred tapped Tink's nose. He gazed at her adoringly.

'Then where are we at?' Tommy stifled a real yawn.

'Are you an early riser?' Jack grinned at him.

'If I have to. Why?'

'Because we are going to search around the tennis court for anything that can be used as a cosh. If you want to become an active part of the investigation, that's your chance.'

'Jolly good.'

'What about me?'

Aunt Mildred touched Uncle Sal's arm. 'I'm afraid we can't afford to be seen behaving in a strange matter. You will have to keep on being a slightly dubious man, and I, the perfect hostess.'

'You said the girl is already rattled.' Judging by the twinkle in Uncle Sal's eyes, he had something up his sleeve, Frances thought.

'She is, and so is her mother.'

'Good. Then it won't take much more to crack her.'

Aunt Mildred agreed. 'I'll let her stew a little, while we're in town. And we shall take Frances along too, to purchase groceries.'

'I'd love that,' Frances said. 'But won't it look funny to have me tag along, when cook gets everything delivered?'

'There's always something we could use. For a dish Mr Bernardo has asked for.'

'What about the suitcase?' Tommy asked. 'It's in my room. If we discover anything, you can take it with you when you see Mr Fitzpatrick.'

'Bring it in here,' his aunt ordered.

They sorted the content into separate piles. Clothes went on one side, toiletries were laid out on a towel, and books and technical publications formed a separate stack.

Because Frances had originally only patted down the clothes, this time she concentrated on checking their seams. A small piece of paper could easily be hidden inside a tie, or an invisible pocket.

Jack went through the books, page by page. Tommy and Uncle Sal concentrated on the wash-bag, including the tins with shaving soap, razor, and facial soap.

Aunt Mildred stared at the unfinished letter. *The party is in full swing, and the weather is clement enough to make one forget the dreariness at home. Maybe we should take a small house here ourselves next winter, you, and me, and Auntie to look after us. The only fly in the current ointment is the constant presence of the same kind of crowd that surrounds me at work. There is a forced artificiality to our gatherings, but I won't bother you with that. Our hostess has invited a new guest, whom I find most intriguing.'*

'What do you make of this?' She showed her nephew the letter.

He laid Agatha Christie's *Murder at the Vicarage* aside to peruse Onslow's writing. 'It's proof, isn't it, that he had his eyes on Uncle Sal? Most intriguing, my hat. More like a gift horse.'

'That's what I thought at first. But then, why draw attention to the fact that there's something peculiar about Sal?' Tink nodded too, as if he and his mistress were a double act.

'At least he appreciated my character work.' Uncle Sal sat a little taller, happy with himself.

'If his sister is at a boarding school in England, it's unlikely she'd read anything into it other than an attempt to amuse her and keep her involved in his life. It's what I would have done.' Jack spoke from experience, as the only one left in his family still in Australia, at least as far as Frances could tell. Neither he nor his mother seemed to be the wiser to where his father lived, after the divorce in Jack's childhood, and neither did they care. She took his hand. She couldn't imagine being abandoned by one's own parent, but it happened. If they ever had children … She stopped herself.

Aunt Mildred set the letter aside. 'Mr Fitzpatrick will want to send this on.'

Jack opened another book, *All Quiet on the Western Front*, by Erich Maria Remarque. 'Onslow had an eclectic taste,' he said.

'He constantly had his nose in a book, when one would encounter him in the club library, instead of just having a quiet drink. It stuck out.' Tommy's face darkened. 'I still can't believe he turned out to be such an utter rotter.'

'Maybe he was hard up,' Jack suggested. 'Then there was the sister to support.'

'I don't care if he had a whole orphanage to feed. One doesn't sell one's country.'

Methodically, Jack checked the pages for clues.

The body of the book looked awfully stiff, Frances thought. 'Take off the dust jacket,' she said.

'It's taped down.'

'Why would he do that?' Uncle Sal grabbed the novel and, inch by inch, used Onslow's nail file to separate the dust jacket from the body of the book. Out fell a small photograph. It showed Fitzpatrick in earnest discussion with another man.

Jack took a closer geek. The second man had a square jaw, and a sallow face. 'I've seen that man before,' he said. 'He was at the Palais de Jetees. I thought Onslow had secretly met with him, but maybe he just spied on him.'

'Because he is the buyer.' Frances could barely contain her excitement.

'But why the photograph? And why is Fitzgerald talking to him?

'Maybe Onslow kept it as an insurance,' Tommy chimed in. 'If anything happens to me, something in that line.'

'Why would the buyer want to kill the goose that lays the golden eggs?'

'That's a question we should definitely ask Fitzpatrick,' Jack said. 'I'd say we're done here for tonight, especially if we're up again before sunrise.'

Tommy gave him a mock salute. 'Yes, sir.'

Frances helped Uncle Sal up and made her way to her own room. They were close to solving the puzzle, she could feel it. And then she and Jack would be free to have fun in the golden riviera sunshine. And Uncle Sal, of course. She still smiled as she fell asleep.

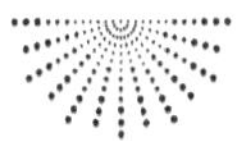

CHAPTER TWENTY

True to his word, Tommy trudged into the kitchen before the break of dawn, only to find Jack and Uncle Sal already waiting, dressed in serviceable flannels. Uncle Sal's pants came courtesy of a trunk of work clothes left behind by other tenants. Frances had shortened the legs with a few stitches. That, and the strong tea she had brewed, was her only contribution for this part of the investigation. She didn't mind, though. After all, she still had her ordinary chores to do, and traipsing around under trees, with the aid of a torch, held little appeal.

She filled Tommy's cup. A blissful look spread over his face as the hot drink woke him up completely. 'What about a bite to eat?'

Frances handed him a bag with sandwiches. 'You can eat them on the way,' she said. 'We don't have much time, and I can't afford to add any more cleaning to my list.' As nice as he was, Tommy tended to make a mess with his food and drinks whenever he was distracted. Or end up staining his clothes. Luckily, he had remembered his failings and settled on a pair of old gray flannels.

She watched them as they stole outside in a single file, with Jack in the lead.

He shone his torch around so Uncle Sal would not trip because of the dark. Although the limp was much less prominent, now they were alone, it was still there. Maybe they should have him see a doctor again.

As if he had read Jack's thoughts, Uncle Sal said, 'Let's slow down a bit.'

'Problems?' Tommy dutifully obliged.

'I tripped over the last step on the staircase. It'll be good-oh again in a few hours.'

At a leisurely pace, they made their way to the tennis-court and the pine tree stand. Needles covered the ground before them, as a last silent reminder of the wild weather the night before.

'What exactly are we searching for?' Tommy's torch light flitted here and there. A bat flew up into the sky, as startled by the humans as they were by the small animal. 'Not a rock, I'd say, and those pines are a bit spindly.'

'He used something smooth.' Jack bade Uncle Sal sit down on a large storage box, to rest his gammy ankle. 'Tree trunks and rocks leave abrasions on the skin unless they're covered in fabric or leather. My best guess is, the killer took one well-aimed whack from behind and knocked him unconscious. Then he did the rest.'

'Isn't it hard to break a neck?' Uncle Sal asked.

'Not if you have an idea what you're doing.' Tommy shuddered. 'Our cook used to demonstrate wringing chickens' necks when I was a toddler. It took me years to be able to eat the birds again.' He wiped the box with his gloved hand before he plonked down next to Uncle Sal. 'Beastly thought, to do that to another man.'

'All the more reason to catch him.' Jack let his light flicker over the ground. He walked deeper into the tree stand, probing the ground for signs of disturbance, and poking into the dense undergrowth.

The smell of pine sap grew strong enough to make him sneeze. Tommy, who worked his way from the other side of the trees towards Jack, followed suit.

'Bless you two,' Uncle Sal sang out.

The first signs of dawn streaked the sky. They'd have to hurry, Jack thought.

Ten minutes later, he'd finished his search. If anything remotely resembling a cosh was hidden here, it had him beaten.

'Let's head back,' he said to Tommy, just as Uncle Sal sang out, 'Come here.'

With perfect sense for the dramatic, the old entertainer flung open the lid of the box he had sat on. Inside, on a folded picnic rug, lay a dozen tennis balls and four rackets. 'Take a closer geek,' Uncle Sal said.

Jack did. The first two appeared to be ordinary, lightweight tennis rackets, suitable for ladies. The third one, heavy enough to act as a weapon, gave its secret away only after Jack examined every inch of the handle by the light of Tommy's torch. A small section of the wood showed a fresh crack.

'It's possible,' Jack said. 'But Frances is right, a rolling-pin from the kitchen or even a billiard cue, cut into two, would have made more sense.'

'Except they might have been missed, and our man could not be sure there would be no blood.' Tommy took the tennis rocket and swung it by the head. 'What a pity dozens of people have used it. Otherwise, we could test it for fingerprints.'

Jack put the racket back and closed the box. 'At least our theory about the pine needles holds up.'

They returned to the house in high spirits. Frances put a finger on her lips as she let them in. 'Geraldine and Mrs Foster will soon be down for their morning tea.'

Silent as mice, Uncle Sal and Tommy tiptoed up the stairs, to their rooms.

Jack hung around. 'Can I help with anything?'

'If you could fetch me another armful of firewood?' She eyed him critically. 'You have a smudge on your face, and on your coat.' She pointed to his sleeve.

'Blast, I have to run and change my clothes then.' He lifted her chin up for a hasty kiss. Frances melted. It was overdue that they could shed their fake roles and be their old selves again.

At breakfast, they were all unusually silent. Geraldine kept her gaze firmly on her plate, and for once the paleness of her face seemed to be natural rather than artificially created. Frances wracked her brain for a way to discover exactly what kind of a favour Mr Bassington-Whyte had asked of the maid. Help her steal something? He'd only have needed to pretend it was some kind of lark. The upper class constantly played silly pranks on each other, according to Mr Wodehouse and other popular authors.

'Frances, are you listening?' Mrs Foster gave her a sharp look.

'Sorry,' she said.

'I said, when you do the shopping, remember to buy ironing starch. I don't expect they will have Robin Starch here, but if they do, please bring me two boxes. Otherwise, a lesser brand will have to do. And we need boot blacking and a shoe brush.'

Frances gulped. 'I don't speak French.'

'I'll write it down for you,' Mr Bowman said. 'All you have to do is give the shopkeepers our list, including the greengrocers'.'

'Thank you.'

'Or I could go,' Geraldine offered. 'Frances is busy enough.'

'Madam said, Frances. Don't you have enough to do with ironing and sewing?' Mrs Foster's smile softened her words.

'It might take a while until we return,' Jack said. 'There's a rattle I don't much care for. It's probably nothing but best to have the local garage take a gander.'

'Please ring us up to keep us informed.' The butler put his napkin aside, a sign that breakfast was over.

'I will. If it takes long, I'll send Madam home in a taxi.'

'And Frances. Cook will need the pine nuts for Mr Bernardo's cake.'

As announced, Jack pulled into the driveway of a small local garage after dropping off Aunt Mildred and Frances at the promenade. He couldn't say why, but the photograph of Fitzpatrick and the stranger had made him uneasy. If anyone wanted to check on their cover stories, it had to be plausible.

To that purpose he had ever so slightly loosened a bolt nut before setting off. It should be easy to find and fix, and even losing it would not cause real harm.

The mechanic gazed lovingly at the gleaming Chevrolet. His hands and his boilersuit were covered in grease and oil, and Jack trusted him instinctively. 'Anglais?' he asked.

'Yes.'

The mechanic nodded. In a mix of French and English they arranged that the mechanic would be only too happy to sort out the problem, and Jack should come back in two hours. Otherwise, he would be welcome to stay and observe.

Jack pointed at his chauffeur's cap. 'I have work to do, but I'll be back.'

He met his friends at a small café at the Place Massena, with a good view of the square. Well-dressed children ran their hands through the water of the fountain, while British nannies watched over them. The local urchins, unsupervised and in frayed shirts and pants, played tag. A few women in heavy dark clothes carried baskets full of shopping – cooks, hastening to their work in restaurants or rented villas, Jack thought. What a feast for the eyes this place was, with its buildings in all colours of the rainbow, bathed in this pellucid light. He pulled himself together.

'The car will take two hours,' he said.

Aunt Mildred's foot tapped impatiently on the floor. "Fitzpatrick and his niece should have arrived already," she said. 'Do you think we should send a boy to their hotel?' They had decided against meeting in Fitzpatrick's room again, before it became too conspicuous.

Jack peered across the square. 'They're on their way.'

'Excuse our delay.' Fitzpatrick pulled up a chair for his niece before he sat down. 'I just received a few more interesting bits of information.'

Jack's gaze flickered over to the grey-haired waiter. 'Is there a more private place to talk? Preferably one where people won't stare if a chauffeur has coffee with his mistress?'

'The museum, next to the Negresco? With any luck there are no other visitors in the house or the gardens. We'll follow you in ten minutes, after our morning coffee.' Fitzpatrick waved at the waiter. 'Café croissant pour deux, monsieur.'

True to his prediction, the neoclassical Villa Massena which now served as a museum, proved to be empty apart from the lady who sold them tickets, and a sad little man with a drooping moustache who ran a listless duster over the marble columns.

Frances held her breath and reached for Jack's hand. As exciting as London was, nothing there had prepared her for this kind of timeless grandeur, with ancient looking friezes running all around the echoing hall.

'The garden is a better idea,' Aunt Mildred said. 'If I remember correctly, it has enough secret places to be unobserved.'

They strolled around on manicured lawns, under yet more palm trees. Frances gazed up to the villa. Uncle Sal would have loved this. She added the museum to the list of places they simply had to explore once they were free.

Aunt Mildred adjusted her large, fashionable sunhat. Frances's cloche felt more unsmart with every minute, but it was just right for a maid, she thought.

Colette waved at them from the entrance to the garden. They met up behind a dense stand of trees. Frances kept to the edge of the group, to act as lookout.

'What have we found out?' Fitzpatrick asked.

'It's likely that Onslow was struck with the handle of a tennis racket and then murdered,' Jack said. 'We found one that fits the bill, and it shows a fresh crack. It would also explain the pine needles the killer lost.'

Fitzpatrick rubbed his neck. 'That's not much.'

'We also found something else, hidden away.'

'The key to the cipher?'

Keeping his gaze unfaltering on Mr Fitzpatrick, Jack slipped his hand into his breast pocket and took out the photograph. 'This one is a bit of a puzzle alright.'

'I don't understand.' Mr Fitzpatrick stared open-mouthed at the picture.

'Onslow kept it well hidden away,' Jack said. 'The question is, who is your mate?'

'He's working in our patent office,' Mr Fitzgerald said. 'Moreover, he's a pilot and the one who sounded the first alarm, when he heard rumours of interest in any kind of promising new invention for aircraft.'

'He tipped you off?'

'He did.' Mr Fitzpatrick handed Jack the photo. 'But it

makes no sense that this photo was in Onslow's possession.'

'Why not?' Frances asked. 'Maybe he was in on it. Would you have come up with a switch for the blueprints without him, even if it didn't go as planned?'

'There would have been no reason.'

Aunt Mildred gave Frances an encouraging nod.

She continued, 'So, if he set the ball in motion and Onslow stole the documents, a picture would have been useful to identify the buyer.'

'Or he could have acted as middleman,' Aunt Mildred added. 'Jack saw him at the Palais de Jetees, him and Onslow.'

'Except he couldn't have taken this picture,' Mr Fitzpatrick said to his niece. 'Did you notice the building in the background, and the heavy overcoats?'

'Let me have a look.' Colette held out her hand. She studied the photo. 'Uncle's right. This picture was taken in October, at the Croydon Aerodrome. I remember packing that coat for you.'

'How can you be sure Onslow wasn't the photographer?' Jack asked.

'Because he spent that month up in Edinburgh. But all the other men on our suspect list could have been there.'

'Don't forget Anne and Lydia,' Colette said. 'There was that frightfully secret technical demonstration you attended, and then afterwards there was the ball at the De Vere.'

'You're right,' her uncle said. 'But that still does not explain why Onslow had that picture.'

'Or why your pilot friend was in Nice that night,' Jack pointed out.

'That could have been perfectly innocent,' Fitzpatrick said.

'That's up to you to find out.' Jack grinned.

Another idea formed in Frances's head. 'What if Onslow found the picture?'

The others stared at her in surprise.

'I mean, what if we got it all wrong? How can we be so sure that Onslow really did steal the blueprints?' She became more and more convinced she was right. 'Maybe he was innocent all along.'

'He had the means, the opportunity, and he searched Uncle Sal's room.' Jack paused. 'I see. If we take his letter to his sister literally, he didn't entirely trust the mysterious Mr Bernardo. It makes sense that he'd want to suss him out in secret. Also, you say Onslow had no idea about the reason he had to take the paper along to work on. What if he did? You said yourself, there were rumours. Onslow was smart, and he had an analytical mind. It wouldn't have been too difficult to put two and two together.'

'Then, instead of being murdered to remove the competition for Uncle Sal's documents, he died because he was close to unmasking the thief. He could easily have searched another room as well that we're unaware of.' Slowly, Mr Fitzpatrick warmed to the theme.

'And that's when he found the photo. He didn't

conceal it because he'd memorised the faces, he hid it because it formed part of his proof.' Frances clapped her hands.

'If only we could be sure that his death and the blueprints are connected.' Aunt Mildred shifted her weight from one foot to another. 'Is there anywhere we can sit down?'

'Soon,' Mr Fitzpatrick said. 'What do you mean?'

'Have you all forgotten Lydia's bracelet?'

Frances groaned.

'I had another chat with the young lady, who again did not feel well enough to come down for breakfast.' Aunt Mildred's dramatic pauses would soon rival Uncle Sal's, Frances thought. What a pity she couldn't follow her youthful dream of a stage career back in the days.

'And?' Mr Fitzgerald prompted her.

'I told her again that I would have to go and see the police, if only to ensure that none of the staff here or the Palais would be falsely suspected of theft.' She allowed herself a moment of self-satisfaction.

Lydia had stared at her as if she had grown hooves and a forked tongue, she recounted. 'She cried out, "but I told you I just lost it." Most unconvincingly, if I may add. I said, that's not the kind of item one loses without anyone finding it. And then the little minx confessed.' She allowed herself a self-satisfied gloat as all eyes were on her.

'What did she do?' Tommy asked.

'They were up to their eyeballs in debt, thanks to Dorothy's foolishness, so the mother had their most valuable jewellery copied, by a terribly clever little man in Hampstead, as she put it.' Aunt Mildred gave Mr Fitzgerald a pointed stare.

'I'll have someone look into him,' he said. 'But lots of people have copies made for harmless reasons.'

'Anyway, Dorothy told the child that, because of all the insurance premiums they had paid over the years, it would be no real loss to the insurance company if they pretended, she had lost the bracelet and claim compensation.' She snorted. 'I told her in no uncertain terms what I thought of that scheme, at which point she had a fit of the hysterics, her mother burst into the room, and I set them both straight. There will be no more shady dealings from those two, and I told Dorothy that I would keep an eye on them.'

'But what does that have to do with Onslow's death?' Jack asked.

'According to Lydia, he saw her take off the bracelet at the Palais and drop it into the water.'

'So, he could either have blackmailed or exposed her,' Jack said. 'I don't think one of the women had the strength or the nerve to snap a neck, but it gives Bassington-Whyte another powerful motive. Money, and saving his family from infamy.'

'At least I could make Dorothy see sense about fraudulent spiritualists. Although, to give credit where it belongs, that woman was clever,' Aunt Mildred said. 'She told Dorothy on several occasions things only she could have known, about her late husband.'

'She did?' Frances oohed.

'Except, one of them was a touching story about their first meeting. I remember hearing it myself on two occasions, and the rest was written in the letters Dorothy kept in her bedside table. Including the bit about the hidden treasure.'

'Interesting, but it is not really clearing up too much,' Mr Fitzpatrick said. 'Even if Onslow is only the victim, and it seems as if Bassington-Whyte has several plausible reasons to want him dead, it is only guesswork.'

'Let us see what we do know.' Jack offered his cigarette case to Mr Fitzpatrick, before he lit a fag.

Mr Fitzpatrick signalled to his niece, who took out her stenographer's pad and pencil.

'If we start with the assumption that Onslow was innocent, then we can rely on his statement when the documents were stolen. We can be reasonably sure that no guest had the opportunity to hand them over to a partner, unless in the house or the garden,' Jack said.

'What about the post?' Frances asked. 'Did anyone have a large letter or a parcel taken to the post office, or does the postman collect them at the door? That could have been the favour Geraldine was taking about, taking care of mail that was supposed to be secret.'

'That would take a lot of trust, to hand over the

merchandise without prior payment, or the other way around.' Jack squinted at her over the smoke spiral.

'If he kept the blueprints, he needed a really safe place for them, where the staff could be sure not to stumble upon them,' she said. 'Maybe in the library or games room? Or in the ball room. Anywhere you can go unseen at night, and where the servants don't spend much time.'

'That's a good idea,' Aunt Mildred said. 'What else can we be sure of?'

'Onslow was smart, but he trusted his murderer.' Jack's tone was final.

'What makes you think that?' Mr Fitzpatrick asked Jack.

'Otherwise, he would never have agreed to meet him outside, at night. But if our man hinted that he had some juicy information about Uncle Sal or something like that, it would make sense.'

'Why were Lady Bassington-Whyte's shoes wet? Maybe she was the one who set up the meeting, and her son did the rest.' Frances's stomach knotted together at the very thought, but it had to be mentioned.

'I certainly hope not.' Aunt Mildred pressed her lips together. 'She said she needed a gasp of fresh air, after Lydia confessed that Onslow might be on to them, and I believe her.'

'Who else had a motive?' Colette made another squiggly note on her pad.

'That depends on the reason, doesn't it?' Jack glanced

around. 'Have you not wondered if there is any other reason to steal an invention that has military uses? Our lads wouldn't be the only posh boys secretly working with the communists.'

'Commies?' Frances had met a few, in Adelaide. They were always the first in line when it came to call for social justice and fair wages and living conditions. Although her boss told them to stop protesting outside the post office, she had the feeling he privately sympathised, as long as they stayed peaceful. So did she.

'These are a bit different from ours,' Jack said. 'They may start out all idealistic and well-meaning, but sooner or later there is bloodshed, and not a little.'

'None of our men has shown any leanings or joined the party,' Mr Fitzpatrick said. 'Also, there are no known contacts to Moscow.'

'You don't need them when half of London is crawling with Russian waiters and taxi drivers, fleeing the revolution. I'm sure France isn't that much different.'

'Let us concentrate on money, before we become all muddled up,' Aunt Mildred said. 'Have you established more about the individual financial situation?'

Colette flipped back a few pages on her pad. 'The Bassington-Whytes urgently need to come up with a little under a thousand pounds. The mother was stupid or desperate enough to see a loan shark in Limehouse, and they're running out of time. They have put the family estate on the market, but it's only a smallish affair in

Northumberland that so far has not attracted any interest.'

Jack stubbed out his cigarette. 'No wonder the son is trying to win a fortune at the gaming tables.'

'At least he isn't cheating at cards,' Mr Fitzpatrick said.

'You mean, he might be a traitor and a murderer, but he still gambles like a gentleman?'

Mr Fitzpatrick had the grace to see the irony as soon as Jack pointed it out. 'It does sound a little stupid.'

'But if Mr Bassington-Whyte stole the blueprints, would he still be as crazy about winning money?' Frances asked.

'That depends on whether he's been paid already, or he could be using it as an explanation why he's suddenly flush.'

'What about the others?' Aunt Mildred peered over Colette's shoulder but gave up as she saw the shorthand.

'Onslow had a steady income of around 500 pounds per annum from bonds that still perform well, plus his income. It's enough to cover the expenses for his serviced flat in Pimlico, the sister's school, and the family home run by his aunt. She's been caring for the siblings since their parents died.'

'No debts, no kept woman, no pressing financial needs?' Mr Fitzpatrick steepled his fingertips together.

'Not unless he spilled out his secrets in his diary,' Jack

said. 'Have your encryption experts come up worth something useful yet?'

'They're still working on the cipher, but it looks more and more as if Frances is right. Onslow was innocent.'

'What about Morris?' Aunt Mildred winced a little as she shifted her weight again.

Colette checked her notes. 'He's run up a few debts, but nothing serious. Fond of Bond street hatters and tailors, but otherwise modest needs.'

'He didn't seem like a dandy to me,' Frances said.

'No, he dresses so conservatively you'd think he has his eyes on a seat in parliament.' Colette clamped her mouth shut as she saw Mr Fitzpatrick's disapproving face.

'An unlikely candidate for excessive greed or communist ideas, then. Unless …'

'Yes, Jack?'

'A person like that would make an excellent secret agent. So inoffensive you wouldn't really pay him any notice, and a first-class mind. Oxford or Cambridge?'

'Cambridge. A first in mathematics, which secured him his current position.' said Mr Fitzpatrick.

'And Jordan?'

'He's got a decent amount in savings, and twice a year he receives income from a Swiss bank. I think he inherited a bundle from his godmother there.'

'Another one not losing sleep over money, then.' Jack grimaced.

'On the contrary, he is definitely well off.'

'And what about Anne?' Frances felt everyone's eyes on her. 'Just because she wouldn't have had the physical strength to commit the murder doesn't mean she couldn't have been involved in any way. Haven't you noticed the way she and Mr Bassington-Whyte look at each other when they think they're unobserved?'

'I only know what everyone knows,' Mr Fitzpatrick said. 'Her family tried to cash in on the stock market and lost it all when the crash came.'

'A girl like that, used to money and the respect that comes with it, and then it's all gone due to something that wasn't her fault, might do something rash to change her fortune.' Aunt Mildred sounded troubled. 'Or she could be tricked into helping a man she's in love with.'

They all nodded.

'What happens now?' Aunt Mildred pulled her shawl tight, as if she was suddenly cold, despite the balmy air. 'Have you made arrangements for the body?'

'Onslow's aunt has been informed by one of our men of the accident,' Mr Fitzpatrick said. 'She was understandably shocked. She asked for him to be cremated here, and the ashes to be brought home afterwards.'

'I see.'

'When is the ceremony going to be?' Jack asked.

'The crematorium has offered us an afternoon spot, the day after tomorrow.'

Francs shuddered. It all sounded so harmless, like booking a restaurant table for afternoon tea.

Jack furrowed his brow. 'Can you arrange it for tomorrow afternoon? We are rapidly running out of time.'

'That should be doable. I assume you have a plan?'

'There is no guarantee that it will work, but I think it might do the trick.'

CHAPTER TWENTY-TWO

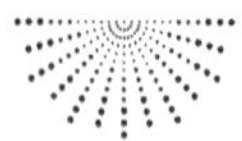

An unfastened shutter banged against the wall. Uncle Sal poked his head out of his window, to see Geraldine leaning out of Lydia's room and grabbing hold of the shutter. He deduced correctly that the young lady had given up hiding in her room.

He gazed down upon the empty terrace and the lawn, which now held three deck chairs on which the young ladies and Jordan sunned themselves. The terrace would have been more convenient, but obviously people didn't feel like being close to the marble staircase.

A soft knock on his door made him pull back his head. Outside his door stood Tommy and Tinkerbell. 'Would you care to join us for a stroll, Mr Bernardo? It'll be easy on your ankle, I promise, and Aunt Mildred wouldn't want you to be cooped up indoors while the old bus is unavailable.' Tommy's face radiated good-natured openness.

Uncle Sal reached for his cane and his silk scarf. 'I am perfectly able to walk for miles. My generation, it is not used to idleness.' He used his stage voice, to project his words without having to raise the volume.

'Oh, absolutely, Mr Bernardo.'

On their way out they passed Bowman, who sorted mail on a silver tray. 'We'll just take a quick dash in the garden,' Tommy said. 'We'll be back in plenty of time for lunch.'

'Very well, sir. Allow me.' Bowman opened the door to the cloak room. 'Will sir want his cape?'

A regal nod from Uncle Sal confirmed that suggestion.

'Well-trained man,' the old entertainer said as soon as they were out of the house and within earshot of the lawn party. 'Has he been with the family long?'

Tommy shrugged. 'Decent staff are a godsend these days, aren't they? You should think people are jolly happy to have a steady job, but most people the agencies send are just not up to snuff. What about you? I assume you left your valet behind when you agreed to come here.'

'I do not like to be tied down,' Uncle Sal said. 'There is always unpleasantness. And snooping.' He wished he could see if any of the listeners reacted to those words, but his role demanded he walk right on.

Tommy gave his friends a helpless shrug and a grimace as they walked past, indicating he only took

Uncle Sal out because he was under orders. Which was perfectly true, only that his orders came courtesy of Mr Fitzpatrick, or just as likely, Jack and Frances.

Tinkerbell ran ahead, threw himself on the ground and rolled around in the grass. 'You want to watch out, Tommy, with that little creature,' Jordan called after them. 'Last week your aunt's mutt wiped his dirty paws all over my flannels.

'As if,' Tommy muttered under his breath. 'Tink knows better than to go where he's not wanted.'

As they reached the tennis court, they both took great care to avoid staring at the box with equipment. Tink ran circles around them, only interrupting himself to sniff at wildflowers or jump at a butterfly.

Uncle Sal paused to rub his ankle.

'Still not better?' Tommy asked.

'It's only the change in weather. Rain always sets it off for a day or two.'

He marched on before Tommy could mention that only in the early hours, Uncle Sal had blamed a misstep. 'How about a rest in the orangerie,' he said. 'Tink is crazy about exploring there, and we are secluded.'

Uncle Sal sat quietly until he caught his breath. The sun cast a golden glow over everything, and dancing fingers of light set Tinkerbell chasing them.

'Here, read this.' Uncle Sal handed Tommy a note which the butler must have hidden in the inner pocket of the cape.

'Right, we're supposed to be gone for at least an hour.' That would leave ample room for a second search of Uncle Sal's belongings, while Bowman kept guard. 'Second, you will receive a phone call during lunch, and on your return to the table, you are to be quietly exhilarated.'

'That's all?'

'I'm afraid so. At least you have an interesting role to play, whereas all I do is grin like a buffoon.' Tommy kicked a flowerpot which fell over.

The more hours passed, the less Frances liked the role she had to play. Lack of sleep, lots of work, and the fact that they most likely spent their nights under the same roof as a ruthless murderer took their toll. The worst part was being unable to talk to Jack and Uncle Sal. Even on their trip to town, Aunt Mildred's company had made it impossible to talk completely freely. Now they were back, she found herself giving a tiny start whenever she heard loud noises.

'Are you unwell?' Mr Bowman asked.

'It's just tiredness.' Frances lined up their purchases. Pine nuts for an Italian cake, boot polish and brush, and two boxes of Robin Starch. The butler's hand touched hers as he took the boot brush. She took the opportunity to palm him a folded note. If Mr Bowman was surprised by her skill, he didn't show it apart from a slight widening of his eyes.

She grinned. Signorina Francesca, talented and lovely assistant of Salvatore the Magnificent, could always be relied on for her performance.

Geraldine clattered towards them. 'You wanted to see me, Mr Bowman?'

'I do indeed. It has come to my ears that you were seen in an intimate discussion with one of the guests.' Frances slipped away, to give them privacy. Also, Mr Bowman was sure to tell them everything about the conversation.

'Wilfred, could you spare me a few minutes?' Aunt Mildred stopped the young man as he bounced downstairs, on his way to lunch. He gave his mother and sister, who followed him in a more staid manner, a perplexed look.

Lady Bassington-Whyte's face turned ashen. Aunt Mildred gave her a comforting shake of her head. 'It's such a beautiful day,' she said to her prey. 'We shall talk in the garden, don't you think?'

He lumbered beside her, his face creased with worry. 'What can I help you with?' he asked as they had reached the terrace.

'Let us walk a little further, where nobody can hear you.'

He followed her, meek as a lamb. If he was their culprit, he was a supreme actor, she thought. But then again, a criminal had to be, if he wanted to evade suspicion.

'That should be enough,' she said after another 100 yards. Even if her guests decided to venture out onto the terrace, she would be able to see them and stop talking. 'It pains me to say this, Wilfred.' She broke off. In her experience, most people would be only too eager to fill in the silence and expand on the unspoken allegation.

He blotted his sweaty face with a handkerchief. 'If it's about my mother or Lydia,' he began.

'No. It's not about them.'

Instead of appearing relieved, he wiped his face again.

'It's about you.'

He gaped at her. 'Me?'

'There are very few strict rules in my house, but those are to be followed, do you understand?' She stomped her foot lightly.

'Yes?'

'One of them is, no corruption of the servants of any kind. You have been seen, Wilfred, skulking around with Geraldine.'

His mouth opened, but no sound came out.

'The maid, Wilfred. That is unacceptable behaviour.'

'It wasn't like that. At all. I swear it on my father's grave.'

'Then please, enlighten me as to what it was. I'd hate

to otherwise have to let Geraldine go, without so much as a reference.'

Geraldine sniffled. 'I didn't do any harm, Mr Bowman. You have to believe me.'

'Then, speak up. What exactly was going on?'

'It's like this. Mr Bassington-Whyte and Miss Anne used to be sweethearts, but nobody was to know for a bit. And then they had a tiff about something, and she didn't want to see him. But he's still carrying a torch for her. So, when Madam invited them both …' She broke off.

The butler scowled at her. 'Spit it out, girl. We have to serve lunch in a few moments.'

'All I did was sneak into her room, after it was made up, and put, like, a flower on her pillow. And once a box of chocolates he bought in Nice, and a few nights ago, the locket she had given back to him. It was ever so romantic.' Her eyes filled with fresh tears. 'I swear, that was all.'

'And what did you receive in return?'

'He said as he might be able to help my boyfriend with a new job. There's his friend's father who runs all these cafés up in Manchester, that are almost as popular as Lyon's, and they need all this baking done.' She gulped for air as she finished the last words.

'You told a guest about your private life?'

'Only because I picked up a handkerchief that he'd dropped. It was one of hers, with that lovely monogram, and he must have held it to his nose to smell the sweet perfume.' Geraldine gave a dramatic sigh. 'He saw straight away that I understood his agony only too well.'

Mr Bowman quelled her with a single glance. 'I'll do my best to explain affairs to Madam, but things like this must not happen again. If you are asked for a secret favour by one of the guests, come to me. Imagine if something had disappeared from Miss Anne's room, and you were seen sneaking inside when you had no reason to go there.'

'Gosh. I never thought of that. Although I did say as I couldn't take any risk, and he said as it was all going to be a breeze.'

'Well, you should have. And now go and wash your face while I ring the lunch gong.'

Aunt Mildred struggled to keep her patience throughout the meal that seemed to drag on. Bassington-Whyte kept his gaze firmly on his plate, his mother kept a worried eye on him, and Lydia toyed with her fish. The other gentlemen ate with a hearty appetite, which still did not speed up affairs.

The butler appeared at Uncle Sal's side. 'A telephone call for sir. Long-distance.'

Uncle Sal rubbed his hands with glee. 'Va bene. You will excuse me.' He hobbled as fast to the door as he could.

'Long-distance? It wouldn't be America, would it?' Tommy speculated.

'Nonsense. It's the middle of the night there,' Jordan said. 'Who knows what these provincial operators consider worthy of that description? Probably anything further away than ten miles.'

'Well, we're very close to Italy, and to Monaco,' Morris said. 'I'd say anything in another country is long-distance, even if it's practically next door.'

'Of course.' Tommy propped up his elbows on the table until his aunt's shocked stare made him sit upright.

'I wish you all would stop this idle speculation,' she said. 'It is none of our business what Mr Bernardo is doing or whom he is conversing with.'

'Yes, Aunt Mildred.' Tommy hung his head.

When Uncle Sal returned a little later, pretend laughter greeted him. He slipped onto his seat with a sly little grin on his lips.

'I hope you found the line acceptable,' Aunt Mildred said in her best hostess manner.

Uncle Sal touched his moustache, as if to hide a wide grin. 'Most satisfactory. Although I might have to take leave of your hospitality for a few hours.'

'Oh.' She raised her eyebrows. 'Will you need Sullivan's services for long?'

'Not at all, dear lady, not at all. Your butler has kindly arranged for a taxi to pick me up within the hour.'

'I see. How very considerate.' She addressed the other guests. 'It has been a dreary time since the incident. I thought maybe a small excursion tonight would cheer us all up? Obviously, not a ball or anything, simply some entertainment away from the villa.'

'Jolly good idea,' Tommy said. 'I for one could do with a spot of putting on the old glad rags.'

'Is it not a bit unseemly?' Lady Bassinton-Whyte blinked owlishly. 'With poor Mr Onslow not even in his grave.'

'He'd want it,' Morris said. 'He was the most considerate chap I've ever met.'

'What's going to happen now, with him?' Lydia's voice wobbled, but her eyes stayed dry.

'His aunt asked for his ashes to be sent home. He'll be quietly cremated tomorrow, with only us in attendance.'

Jordan cocked his head at her in sympathy. 'You're a tower of strength, Mrs Clifton.'

'One tries. But first, we shall have a little bit of fun tonight.'

After lunch, the men went outside for a smoke. 'Tommy?' Aunt Mildred waved him back. 'Right-ho,' he said and trotted inside again.

When he joined his friends again, his mood had changed to glum.

'What's up?' Morris asked. 'Tummy-ache? I have bicarbonate of soda in my room. Although I'm actually feeling swell. Top-notch cook you have here.'

'I'm fine,' Tommy said. 'Just saddled with a few more rather unpleasant tasks to do with tomorrow.'

Jordan sucked the air through his teeth. 'Better you than the old gal. Mind you, your aunt is very sporting and all that, but certain things should be left to us men.'

'Anyway, I should be back for afternoon tea. If I'm late, save me a slice or two of Bernardo's cake. One gets a bit tired of scones and crumpets.'

'We'll guard it with our lives,' Bassington-Whyte said. The others grimaced at his unlucky choice of words.

'What are you going to do while I'm gone?'

'Nothing much. Shoot a game of billiards, or go down to the tennis court.' Jordan shrugged. 'If you run into the Bernardo fellow, keep an eye on him. I lay you a tenner that fellow's a wrong 'un.'

'My thinking exactly.' Tommy ambled off.

Jack picked him up just after Uncle Sal had set off in a secretive manner, with a small briefcase in his hands. The taxi driver had announced his arrival with a satisfactory honk, thus alerting everyone.

'Follow that taxi,' Tommy said in his best Sherlock Holmes imitation.

'We'll stick to them alright.' Jack switched into

second gear as they drove past the gates and onto the road. 'Do you think they bought into Uncle Sal's act?'

'They swallowed it hook, line, and sinker. You should have seen him at lunch. He positively oozed self-satisfaction.'

They came onto the meandering main road, which afforded them expansive views of the glittering Mediterranean Sea. Although there was little traffic at this hour, Jack kept the speed at a maximum of thirty miles, out of respect for the sudden bends and tight corners, and because he wanted to savour the beauty of the trip.

Monte Carlo was busier than Nice had been, or maybe it only seemed this way because of its compact size. Yachts and fishing boats lined the piers, and weather-toughened men with cigarettes stapled to their mouth, neckerchiefs and striped jerseys emptied baskets full of catch and scrubbed decks.

Jack parked the Chevrolet away from the water, high up in the old town. Even so, they could easily walk down to the palm-lined promenade within a quarter of an hour. For now, though, Tommy led him to a small, cobbled alley, lined on both sides by lemon-coloured buildings. As unlikely as it was to run into an acquaintance away from the main attractions, they could not risk it.

A gloved hand waved at them from behind the cover of a newspaper. Mr Fitzpatrick had arrived early enough to secure a secluded table, and coffee, pastis and a bottle of water. Uncle Sal joined them a little later. He leant on his cane as he climbed up the steep alley.

Jack studied him with concern. Uncle Sal winked at him. 'Don't let my old man act fool you, my boy. It's just easier to stay in character if I don't want to slip up.' He sniffed at the bright green pastis. 'Strong stuff, eh?'

'If you're not used to it, it can knock you over after a few glasses.'

'In that case, I'll stick with coffee. We all need a clear head tonight.'

Mr Fitzgerald sipped his drink. 'Just one for me, to blend in. People remember stingy foreigners.'

'Is everything in place for the next part?' Jack asked.

'I certainly hope so,' Uncle Sal said. He patted the briefcase. 'In exactly fifteen minutes the chauffeur will pick me up outside the bank. The moment we see him, I'll enter the building, with this briefcase.'

'I'll wait for you,' Mr Fitzpatrick said. 'The safe deposit box is rented under the name Monsieur Bernard, the key is in my pocket, and all we have to do is put the briefcase into the box and have you leave the bank with empty hands.'

Uncle Sal pushed himself upright. 'At my speed, we should go. It's no denying I'm dragging my chains like billy-oh.'

He chortled as he saw Mr Fitzpatrick's unnerved expression. 'No worries, I'll switch the Australian lingo for my Italian side as soon as we bring this show on the road.'

'Break a leg.' Jack drained his coffee cup in two big swills.

Uncle Sal left first, with Mr Fitzpatrick close enough to protect the old man from possible thugs who might think a lame person was an easy target, yet far enough to make it seem as if they were unconnected.

'And now?' Tommy asked.

'Now we wait until we can be sure that Uncle Sal is back way ahead of us. Is there any place of interest close by?'

'The more we're out and about, the likelier it is to be spotted. How about we stay here?'

When they came home, Tommy regretted having downed what felt like a gallon of coffee. His stomach heaved at the smell of tea and he wanted nothing more than an hour or two of rest.

'Hullo, everyone,' he cried out nevertheless as he entered the drawing room, where the whole company with the lone exception of his aunt was assembled. He let his gaze wander over the table. Plates full of crumbs, a lonely scone, and a few slices of toast were all that was left. 'What happened to my cake?'

'Sorry, old chap.' Jordan gave him a playful shrug. 'It proved to be a little too irresistible for the rest of us.'

'Torta della Nonna.' Uncle Sal sliced off a forkful from the thick slab on his plate. 'The Grandmother's cake is well known to be impossible to stop after only one little piece.'

'It's your own fault for driving off without offering us a lift.' Lydia pouted in a droll manner that indicated a joke.

'I'm sure there were good reasons,' interjected her brother. 'Would you like a bite or shall we leave the ladies in peace?'

'By all means, let us go.' Tommy rang for the butler. 'Please tell my aunt that I'm back and that I have made the dinner arrangements. If she needs me, I'll be in the games room.'

'Without me.' Uncle Sal enjoyed another forkful of cake. 'I shall enjoy the company of the beautiful ladies instead.'

Lady Bassington-Whyte giggled, and both Lydia and Anne moved a little closer to Uncle Sal.

'What do they all see in this chap?' Bassington-Whye asked in a peevish manner as they settled in the games room.

'Well, he does possess a certain cosmopolitan charm, my aunt says.' Tommy chalked up a cue. 'Anyone for a round?'

Jordan set up the rack. 'I thought she didn't trust him.'

'She doesn't. She only said she can't help liking him.'

'Anything interesting on your trip?' Bassington-Whyte flung himself into a chair.

The carelessness was a little exaggerated, Tommy thought, but a casual observer would not guess the man to be in any sort of tight spot. He signalled Jordan to take the break shot.

'You've got stripes,' Jordan said after the balls came to a halt.

Tommy took good aim. 'We followed Mr Bernardo to Monte Carlo,' he said.

'What?' Morris jaw dropped. 'Wouldn't Sullivan think that awfully strange?'

'No, because I'd heard where our man told his chauffeur to go, so I just gave Sullivan an address, without any explanation.'

He sank the ten and the eleven, before he missed a shot.

Jordan took over. 'What happened then?'

'Our pigeon went into a bank.' Tommy chalked the tip of his cue again, his gaze lowered so he could discreetly watch for reactions. 'When he went in, he carried the briefcase. When he came out, he didn't.'

Jordan missed as Morris whistled loudly. 'That is weird.'

'You want to hear what's even more interesting?' Tommy waited for a heartbeat. 'The briefcase was empty.'

'What are you saying?' Jordan put the cue stick aside.

'He borrowed it from my aunt, and I kept him in my sight from the moment she gave it to him until he climbed into that taxi. You know what I think?' Tommy lowered his voice in a conspiratorial manner. 'I believe he used the thing as an excuse to rent a deposit box.'

'For what reason?'

'I have no idea. Yet. But I've booked a table at the Hotel de Paris in Monte Carlo for tonight. It's an easy stroll to the casino afterwards and I for one intend to keep an eye on our interesting friend.'

'Capital idea,' Morris said. 'We could take turns, to make it more natural. Teams of two?'

CHAPTER TWENTY-FOUR

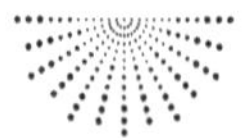

To avoid any wait for the rest of the party, Tommy had also hired a taxi, which carried the ladies and Uncle Sal to the restaurant. Jack chauffeured the rest. They were dining unfashionably early, but it felt more decorous with regards to current events, Aunt Mildred had said.

During the drive, Tommy noticed how much effort everybody put into no longer mentioning Onslow. Quite soon he'd be relegated to vague memories of somebody one hadn't known terribly well.

He wondered if Reginald Fitzgerald suffered any kind of remorse. After all, it had been his scheme that had gone awry, and Onslow had been an innocent pawn.

'You're a trifle pale around the gills, old bean,' said Bassington-Whyte.

'What? Sorry, just trying to figure out if I forgot anything on my aunt's list today.'

'Bit late now,' Morris said. 'My method is, plan things in the correct order and tick them off accordingly. Works a treat.'

A sleek, dark green Lagonda behind them honked. It swerved wildly as it overtook their Chevrolet. In the glare of their headlights, they could spot a tipsy couple toasting them with a flask.

Jack gripped the steering-wheel tight.

'Now that car's the bee's knees,' Bassington-Whyte said with awe.

'Not if you drive like that oaf,' Jordan said. 'I'll lay you a tenner they won't make it any further than Cap d'Ail, if they don't slow down.'

'I'm not throwing my money away,' Morris said. 'Bassington-Whyte is right. The Lagonda is a sweet bus. You should get one, Jordan. You're the only one here rich enough to afford it.'

'And give up my evening tipple? Unless I hire someone like Sullivan here.' He leant closer to Jack, and Tommy on the passenger seat. 'What do you think of this little party? A bit on the quiet side, maybe?'

'I find it all very pleasant, thank you.' Jack made way for another car, with yet another very happy couple.

'I'd say there is a proper party going on somewhere,' Morris said.

'I didn't know you were that keen on the wild stuff.' Tommy chortled, good-naturedly.

'I'm not. Just wondering who these folks belong to.'

'They were French, weren't they?'

'Or Italian. Half of Monaco hails from that country.'

'Maybe that's why Bernardo went there.' Jordan drummed his fingertips on the back of Tommy's seat.

Jack dropped off his passengers outside the Hotel Paris. A liveried doorman hastened to open the doors for them.

Tommy handed Jack a few banknotes. 'Get yourself a bite to eat, and don't forget to come to the Casino. I'm sure there will be a room where you can wait.'

'Thank you, sir.'

Jack squeezed the Chevrolet into a tight spot by the pier, next to the Lagonda, which now showed a dent in the door.

Streetlamps cast their light onto the promenade, and out over the silvery water. The heady scent of flowers mingled with the salty sea air in a way that made Jack suddenly long to be back home. Although he couldn't have wished for a more reliable second-in-command than his old sergeant Bluey, and Bluey's capable wife, a lot of things could go wrong without him there to fix then. Most of all, he missed their company. If he felt like this, how must Frances feel, cut off from everyone thanks to her role as a housemaid?

Frances wished Jack were by her side, or Uncle Sal, as she crept out of her room. At least she had the butler to help her snoop around the library and the games room.

'Is that you, Frances?' Geraldine poked her head out of Foster's room where the two had their work cut out for them, mending and ironing clothes for everyone ahead of tomorrow's cremation. 'Can you bring us more hot water for the iron?'

'Good-oh. I won't be a jiff.' Frances hurried downstairs and into the kitchen. It smelt faintly of the bar soap they used to scrub the floor and the stove, and the dishes were all done. To Frances delight, Madame Petit had already retired for the night, so Bowman was her only company on this floor.

She put the kettle on to boil. It left her with nothing to do but think as she waited. They had too many suspects, and too little to go on. If Jack's idea failed, they were out of options. Unless –

Mr Bowman's silent entrance gave her a start. 'I'm sorry,' he said. 'I was wondering where you were.'

The kettle whistled. Frances filled a thermos and carried it up.

Mr Bowman had already embarked on his search of the library. Despite its grandiose name, it contained only two bookcases and a basket full of magazines and newspapers. The desk blotter was replaced regularly, the drawer was open to everyone, and Frances had lifted the rug this very morning, to sweep the floor underneath.

She knelt to feel under the chairs for anything taped to them while Mr Bowman used a torch to shine behind the bookcases.

'Where would you keep the papers?' she asked the butler. After all, if his real job was with the intelligence service, he would have a lot of experience.

'Somewhere I can instantly lay my hands on them,' he said without hesitation.

'Which he could do here, or in the games room, except other people might come in.' Frances rose. 'What about the ball room?'

'It's locked.'

'Even better for him. Do you have the key? Otherwise, I'll have to run up to my room.' Uncle Sal had given in and handed over the skeleton keys.

He dangled his key ring.

Frances stopped in the hallway. The ball room lay opposite Aunt Mildred and Tommy's suites and backed onto their bathroom. It would take a lot of bad luck to be noticed, breaking into this room.

She stepped aside so Mr Bowman could unlock the door. Inside, she drew in her breath, overcome with awe at the splendour. The gleaming crystal chandelier was reflected in half a dozen mirrors, and candles were stuck in the wall sconces between them. Upholstered divans and chairs stood in a half circle around a grand piano, fronting the dance floor.

'Where shall we begin?' she asked, suddenly remembering not to appear too impressed. After all, she'd spent enough time at the "Top Note", which without any doubt was the most spiffing nightclub in all of Australia, and she had travelled halfway around the world on a posh ocean liner.

'With the furniture.' He lifted a scatter cushion and prodded it with gentle fingers.

They were close to giving up, when Frances opened the piano. Inside, a stack of sheet music caught her eye. She picked it up. Hidden between the musical scores were two smaller sheets of paper, with what looked like frightfully technical drawings. Her heart drummed a jubilant staccato. 'I think we found it.'

Mr Bowman stared wide-eyed at the papers. 'I can't believe it. I honestly thought we'd never see these blueprints again. That is –' He checked the sheet music again, turning each page with the utmost care.

Frances's heart sank. She'd been so proud of herself, and now, Mr Bowman's face grew more and more disappointed. 'Are they fakes?'

'No, not at all. It's just that the first two pages are missing. Anyway, we need to let the boss know.'

'Have you checked the envelope in Mr Bassington-

Whyte's room? Although it would be barmy to keep the two pages there.'

'I did have a peek,' he admitted. 'He keeps letters from Miss Lydia in that envelope .'

She played with her headband which had come undone. 'You could ring Mr Fizgerald up,' she said. 'He might still be at his hotel.'

After a glance at his watch, Mr Bowman shook his head. 'He'll be with your Jack now.'

'Then ring up the bar where they're meeting and have them call Jack,' she suggested. 'Surely there's nothing suspicious about the head of the household staff asking to speak to a chauffeur. If I keep watch, you can use the telephone in this house. That's much easier than you having to cycle a long way.'

He broke into a sudden laugh. 'I wish we could hire you. We certainly could do with someone as clever as you three.'

She curtsied. 'Why, thank you ever so kindly, sir,' she said in her best humble servant tone.

Before Mr Bowman placed the call, Frances slipped upstairs. From Madame Petit's room came a comforting, regular snore.

She opened the door to Mrs Foster's room wide enough to glimpse inside. Foster and Geraldine were still busy with their ironing and so engrossed, they did not notice her.

Nevertheless, she kept standing guard by the open

door, as Mr Bowman spoke on the phone in the hall. He hushed his voice. 'Yes, two of the four parcels have not yet been sent off.' He paused, probably waiting for instructions, Frances guessed. 'Very good. I shall let Madam know as soon as she has returned.' He rang off.

'What did he say?' Frances asked.

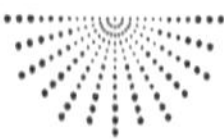

ack hung up the receiver and thanked the bartender. His mind churned as he signalled Mr Fitzgerald to meet him outside. They had settled the bill as soon as their drinks had come, so nobody could find their behaviour curious.

'Two pages?' Mr Fitzgerald frowned. 'That's peculiar.'

'That's what I thought at first, but what if it was an instalment? He must have sent off the first two, to be verified, and the other two were to follow after he'd been paid.'

'Possibly. But how would he send them out? Even if, and that is a big if, Onslow had kept quiet about the loss, it would be obvious that there were no blueprints among his belongings. In which case the handover would become difficult if it were to be affected before the party travelled home.'

'Who says it would have to happen in Nice?' Jack pieced the things together in his mind.

'If not here, then why not steal them back home in Whitehall?'

'I believe that France was chosen for a good reason. But what I would have done is, board the train with the others, go for a drink in the bar or bump into another passenger on a corridor and palm him the documents. I assume the travel arrangements were well known in advance?'

Mr Fitzgerald nodded.

'It might be worth a try to get hold of the passenger list, and to have a man at every railway station, to see whoever gets off the train.'

'I'll take care of it. Except – what do we do about the documents? If our man slips through our fingers, we'll have lost the invention for good.'

'You won't. We'll replace those two pages with something that'll hold up for just long enough to convince our thief he got away with it.'

There was a moment's pause before Mr Fitzpatrick clapped Jack on the back. 'Capital idea. We'll use our own forgery to pull off the exchange.'

'Exactly. I assume you have a set at your disposal?'

'I had a copy couriered over right after the theft, to be on the safe side.'

'In that case, I'll have Bowman switch them over as soon as everyone's asleep.'

He glimpsed towards the brilliantly lit Casino where Aunt Mildred's party approached as they spoke. 'You've got two hours until the next bit.'

'It's all going to run like clockwork,' Mr Fitzpatrick promised. 'If Mr Bernardo can work his magic.'

'Well, hello there.' Jordan and Bassington-Whyte had gone to the bar, to order a round of champagne cocktails for the ladies, when they became aware of a golden-haired beauty giving them a little finger flutter. Jordan promptly abandoned his friend and approached the lady, who was already surrounded by a bevy of admirers. He bent over her hand. 'How delightful to find you here, Miss Colette.'

She gave him a bewitching smile. 'Please, drop the miss.'

'Would you care to join us at the baccarat table?'

'Maybe in a little while. The cards haven't been nice to me at all.' She craned her neck. 'There's Tommy, and I forgot the other name.' She waved them closer.

'What a smashing luck to run into you,' Tommy said. 'Would you like another drink? Although I don't think they'll have your Cat-A-Tonic.'

Her laughter rang out in a silvery peal, very unlike the

efficient Colette with the shorthand skills and brisk movements he had met in her uncle's room.

'How darling of you to remember. This is almost my last evening, and my purse is no closer to being full enough to get that beastly bartender to part with his recipe, so I'll have a Mimosa.'

'In that case we'll have to do our best to assist your luck,' a gooey-eyed Morris said. His behaviour took Tommy by surprise. He had never seen the placid young man act like this over a girl.

'What do you say, Bassington-Whyte?' Morris asked. 'Shall the young lady be our good luck charm, and we'll cut her in on our wins?'

'It's a bit rum, but I promised mother I'd keep her and the rest of the ladies company,' Bassington-Whyte said.

Jordan rolled his eyes. 'But surely you won't be tied to her apron-strings all night.'

An angry red colour appeared on Bassington-Whyte's cheek bones, yet another reaction Tommy had not expected. The evening promised to be most interesting.

'I wouldn't dream of breaking up your party,' Colette purred.

'Not at all.' Jordan offered her his arm. 'Be a sport and bring the drinks, Clifton.'

'Where's your other friend? Peter, was it?' The young woman gave them an artless smile.

The silence felt oppressive, Tommy thought, although in reality it couldn't have been more than a few seconds before Morris piped up. 'I'm afraid he had to leave us early.'

'What a shame. And what about your charming Mr Bernardo? I hope he didn't have to leave as well.' Colette put her gloved hand in the crook of Jordan's arm and let him sweep her off towards the baccarat table.

Uncle Sal was in great form as he and the ladies toured the gilded rooms, which were adorned with precious tapestries and paintings, fit for a king. He regaled the ladies with stories about the fabled casino, the opera and the concert hall at the front of the palais that were a big part of Monte Carlo's cultural life.

'I remember Dame Nellie Melba, performing under this very roof,' he reminisced. 'The crowd was so quiet I could hear my own heart pound at the sheer beauty of that sweet voice. Then, as one man, we all rose from our chairs, we rose, and we clapped until the hands, they were too delicate to pick up the cards.' He chuckled. 'Alas, I was not too delicate to pick up the chips for the roulette.'

'Did you win?' Lydia's eyes sparkled, and her azure blue dress made her appearance all the more striking in the blue and golden casino rooms. She lounged on a gilt chair and seemed to have overcome any fear over their fraud attempt or Onslow's death.

'Monte Carlo has always been a lucky place for me,'

Uncle Sal said, as Tommy and the others arrived in the wake of Colette and Jordan. 'Have you ever heard of the night when many patrons lost millions of francs, betting on red, because they foolishly thought that the ball cannot fall on black for too long without a break?'

'Were you there? Did you win?' In her excitement, Lydia clasped Uncle Sal's sleeve.

'I was. It was the year before the war, but I am a cautious man. I trust in luck, but I also believe that it takes more than a small ball to make your fortune.' Uncle Sal gave Lydia an elaborate wink before he took Colette's hand and kissed it with all the elegance he could muster. 'You, bella Signorina, together with Signorina Lydia and Signorina Anne, outshine the stars tonight.'

Lydia and Anne both giggled at the extravagant compliment. Colette again broke into her silvery laughter. 'If your touch at the gambling tables is half as golden as your tongue, Mr Bernardo, I'd be happy to let you place my bets at the roulette.' She half-turned to Jordan and Morris. 'Shall we tempt fate?'

They swept her off between them. Lady Bassington-Whyte whispered a few words into her son's ear. Aunt Mildred told Tommy they did not need him, and to keep Mr Bernardo entertained.

'Shall we have a little flutter ourselves?' she asked. 'The Trente Quarante Salle is usually a wonderful place where you meet the more interesting people.' She rubbed her hands together in happy anticipation.

'I'm not much for gambling, but I used to be a dab hand at this game.' Lady Bassington-Whyte sipped her cocktail.

'Papa used to say you're a fiend at Trente e Quarante.' An excited pitch crept into Lydia's voice.

'Are the stakes very high?' Anne bit her lip.

'Don't worry, my dear.' Aunt Mildred glanced around, to make sure they were unobserved as she opened her evening bag. Inside was a large handful of 50 and 100 francs chips. 'They belonged to Mr Onslow, may his soul rest in peace. His aunt is opposed to gambling. She said I should put them to good use.'

'We could try to win and afterwards donate whatever these chips were worth to an orphanage, in his memory.' Lady Bassington-Whyte's gaze was glued to the riches in Aunt Mildred's bag.

'I'm sure he would have approved,' Anne said. 'The poor pet was generous.'

'Then let us proceed.' Aunt Mildred allowed herself a mental pat on the back. If Lydia and Anne wouldn't pass on this information to young Bassington-Whyte, then Tommy would spread the news, including a little nugget she kept to herself for the moment.

The Trente Quarante Salle had a fair number of people seated around its tables, but nothing compared to the crowds attracted by the roulette wheels in their room.

Most of the gamblers were of an advanced age, but a group of young men attracted Lydia's attention.

'I'll watch from the sidelines,' she said to her mother and pecked her on the powdered cheek. 'Good luck, Mamma.'

Jack toyed with his wine. He had ordered a bottle of red, in the only bar that allowed him a glimpse of the casino garden where the next act would play out. He took out the photograph showing Fitzgerald and the sallow man again. This time, though, he focussed on the composition.

In his mind, he erased the background, and the angle that showed the photographer had been unable to use a tripod or get close to his subjects. Or his subject. While his companion's face had a blurred quality, Fitzpatrick's features showed up clear enough to be easily recognisable. Which meant, unless Fitzpatrick was the culprit, a notion that Jack dismissed, it must have been used as a warning to stay away from that man. That underlined their suspicions. All the men in the house party could easily have come across him in Whitehall. It might also explain why Onslow had not reached out to Mr Fitzgerald. He was unsure who he could trust.

'Monsieur Jacques?' A wiry young waiter called out toward Jack's table.

'That's me.'

'There is a message for you. You are needed.'

'Thank you.'

He made his way, not towards the garden, but to the entrance to the casino where Aunt Mildred awaited. Her face was flushed, either with the heat in the palais, or with anticipation.

'Bring the car around in thirty minutes, please,' she said. 'I hope I'll find Mr Bernardo in time.'

Through the open doors. Jack caught a glimpse of Colette and her admirers as they headed for the bar. He raised his voice slightly.

'I may be mistaken, but I think I saw Mr Bernardo with his friend taking the air by the waterfall.'

'In the garden? Are you certain?'

He raised his hands in an apologetic manner. 'All I saw from my table outside the bar was a limping gentleman in a top hat, with an opera cape and a cane, and another gentleman at his side.'

'I see. Thanks. Sullivan.'

He tipped his finger to his cap. 'Madam.'

Aunt Mildred sailed majestically towards the entrance to the garden. 'Wait up,' Tommy called out close to her. 'Where are you going?'

'Searching for Mr Bernardo. Unless he's turned up?'

Tommy shook his head. 'Not since he mumbled something and slipped out of the room.'

'How very vexing. Sullivan believes he saw him in the garden, but I'm not sure how clear his view really was from a distance.'

'I'll hunt for him. The place is a bit of a jungle, and it isn't frightfully well-lit. We don't want you to turn your ankle,' Tommy said.

'There is no need for your concern. I am in perfect shape.' She played with her pince-nez.

'Of course, jolly good,' he hastened to add.

'Nevertheless, I would appreciate your assistance. And then you can tell the others to gather their coats, as we shall leave at midnight.'

She marched off, towards the Trente Quarante Salle, where Lady Bassington-Whyte had been torn between the card table, and the pleasing view of her daughter enjoying a mild flirtation with an American gentleman who reeked of wealth.

To Aunt Mildred's relief, they had come out ahead with their gambling, although Mr Fitzgerald's ministry would be easily able to absorb the loss of the money purportedly forming part of Onslow's estate.

'Look who I found.' Tommy tapped her on the shoulder. A quick glance at Uncle Sal, and his whereabouts became obvious. There were a few crumbs of dark soil on his shoes, and a leaf hung onto his pant leg.

'Have you seen the garden yet?' Uncle Sal beamed at her like a benevolent cherub. 'It is bellissimo. The palais is awash in a thousand lights, the stars sparkle like diamonds and –'

'Most delightful, I'm sure,' she said. 'But maybe a little unwise, to wander around alone. My nephew just reminded me how easy it is to have a mishap, and nobody with you to call for help.'

'Your concern touches my heart.' He patted his chest to emphasise how deeply affected he was. 'I only wanted a little solitude, a moment to commune with my soul.'

'What a load of hoodwink,' Tommy told his friends as they waited for Jack to pick them up. Because she held more than a thousand francs of winnings in her bag, Aunt Mildred had allowed herself to be persuaded not to put any trust in a taxi driver who might be in cahoots with armed robbers. Despite any lack of evidence, Lady Bassington-Whyte held forth on the subject until her daughter begged her to be quiet. Uncle Sal had offered his company, too, as a second man in case there should be an unfortunate incident.

'What are you talking about?' A dimple appeared in Colette's cheek.

'Nothing,' Jordan said. Morris nodded, mesmerised by Colette. The chap really held a torch for her, Tommy decided.

She hid a yawn behind her hand. 'Would it be too utterly rude if I left you?' She swung her evening clutch which, although less heavy than Aunt Mildred's, contained a healthy cut of their winnings.

Morris goggled at her. 'How are you getting home?

What do you say, Tommy, shall we have Sullivan take Colette to her hotel?'

'That's sweet of you, but, honestly, I've promised a friend to meet for a nightcap and she'll either offer me a bed for the night or have her car take me. You see, there's nothing to worry about.' An even bigger smile produced the dimple again.

'So, it's good-bye?' Morris' features took on a hangdog expression.

'I'm afraid so. But maybe we'll run into each other again. I might look you up in Whitehall when I'm next in London.' She blew them a kiss and sashayed out of the room.

Jordan gave him a playful punch. 'That is an amazingly pretty squeeze.'

Morris stiffened. 'I'll ask you to speak a little more respectful of the lady. Right, chaps?

'What, who? Yes. Remarkably pretty.' Bassington-Whyte turned on his heel. 'Who's coming with me to the bar while we wait?'

'I think I'll stick to coffee,' Tommy said.

'Good idea.'

They chatted about nothing much until a page boy came to tell them their car was ready.

Tommy climbed into the passenger seat as the other three squeezed themselves into the back. It must have been even tighter with Uncle Sal and four women to drive. 'I say, Sullivan?'

'Yes, sir?' Jack eased the Chevrolet onto the road.

'You mentioned that you spotted Mr Bernardo in the garden. You must have eyes like an eagle, if it was him.'

'A good chauffeur learns how to recognises his charges, sir. I'm quite sure it was him.'

'Amazing how one runs into old acquaintances at the Riviera,' Jordan took over. 'Like Miss Colette tonight. Was Mr Bernardo's friend as much of a looker? I've heard he's quite the ladies' man.'

'I wouldn't know about that, Mr Jordan. In any case, he met with a man. I got a decent eye-full of them because the waterfall caught the light from the Palais.'

'Someone we know?' Tommy turned around and winked at his friends.

'Not that I'm aware. A couple of inches taller than Mr Bernardo, with a sallow face.'

'It's that artificial light that makes folks look sickly,' Tommy suggested.

'He was standing face to face with Mr Bernardo, and there was no mistaking his sallow skin.' Jack had decided against throwing in the fact about the square jaw. 'Ask Mr Bernardo.'

'Gosh, no.' His own laughter rang fake in Tommy's ears. 'It's none of our beeswax, only a bet we had going among ourselves.'

r Bowman opened the door for the gentlemen. He gave Jack a quick nod, to dismiss him.

Jack grinned to himself as he unlocked the garage and put the Chevrolet away for the night, after taking out the distributor cap again. Then he settled in with his sketchpad and pencil while he waited.

It was past two when soft raps on the door alerted him to Mr Bowman's arrival. 'Sorry it took so long.' The butler closed the door behind him. 'I needed to be sure they're all asleep.'

'I'm used to late hours.' Jack took a stiff envelope from the Chevrolet's luggage trunk. 'If you hand over the originals, I'll pass them on to your boss.'

'It's a rum go, this whole affair.' Mr Bowman lit a cigarette. 'If only our bird had the courtesy to go and steal Mr Bernardo's top secret documents, so we could clap him in irons.'

'We'll make it worthwhile for him to come out of the woodworks.'

'I suppose so, but I can't say I like it. There's too many ifs involved, and too many people.'

'Trust us. We've done this before.'

'Oh, I have faith in you. But the Cliftons? I know young Tommy's type. Brave, and well-meaning, but there's always a little of distaste for anything he'd consider not quite cricket. The same goes for his aunt.

Plucky, and a good sport, but not really up for underhanded tricks.'

Jack guffawed. 'You haven't seen those two in action yet. If your people are half as good, consider yourself lucky.'

'In that case, I'll gladly stand corrected. By the way, your young lady sends her love. A game girl, that. But I should push off now.'

The tick of the grandfather clock, by day nothing but a pleasant background noise, took on an ominous loudness as the butler padded up the servants' stairs. Every nerve in his body was alert and he paused with every step, to avoid any noise. In the ballroom, he tried to remember the exact position of the documents in the sheet music.

He swore silently under his breath. What was wrong with his memory? He fished for his handkerchief, to wipe his brow. A crinkle in his pocket gave him a start. He pushed his hand deeper inside and brought out a slip of paper, with a handwritten note. *'Madam's requests for gramophone records: Let's Do It (Let's Fall in Love) by Cole Porter and Someday I'll Find You by Noel Coward.'*

With infinite care, he slipped the falsified documents into the slots specified by the note. Bless Frances's ingenuity, he thought, as he crept away and locked the room again.

For once, there were no stragglers at breakfast, yet Aunt Mildred was uneasy. and she pushed her scrambled eggs around on the plate without eating.

'Is anything wrong?' Tommy asked, every inch the doting nephew. He helped himself to two rashers.

'Please tell us if there's anything we can do,' added Jordan as he spread lashings of butter on his golden toast.

'It's probably a ridiculous notion and you'll think me a fool.'

'Never,' Uncle Sal proclaimed. 'Do tell us, my dear lady.'

'It's this.' She paused until everyone paid her their full attention. 'When I had the new maid pack up Mr Onslow's belongings, there was a photographic camera. A very valuable German model, I presume.'

'Did she damage it? That would be a shame. These German cameras are said to be top of the tree, but I could have a gander.' Morris's eyes gleamed.

'She did no such thing, and of course the apparatus will be sent to his heirs, together with everything else.' Aunt Mildred creased her brow deeper.

'Then I don't see the problem.' Tommy cut off a piece of bacon and chewed heartily.

'There is a film roll inside, and it appears, pictures were taken. The question is, should I have them developed here in Nice, to avoid any unpleasant surprises? Or would any of you know what kind of photographs Mr Onslow used to take? I don't think his aunt would be happy if it turns out he had a fondness for, shall we say, bathing beauties.'

Bassington-Whyte blew out his cheeks until his mother's icy glare stopped him. 'I say, that is a bit of a puzzler. I hadn't the foggiest he had a photographic camera.'

'I don't think Onslow would have had any interest in naughty pictures, but your idea of making sure the poor aunt won't have to deal with more upsetting things is the right thing,' Morris said. 'If you want me to, I can remove the film and we could drop it off at a local studio when we go to Nice this afternoon.'

Aunt Mildred shot him a grateful smile, without making any commitment.

'I don't understand,' Frances said to Tommy as she came in to tidy his room after breakfast. 'Unless the person we're after has a correct film roll handy, he couldn't replace it. If he steals it, it's obvious what happened, especially because everybody got the news about the film.'

'According to Jack, that's not when he will strike.' Tommy scratched his clean-shaven chin. 'I must say, this is all dashed exciting, as sad as the whole affair is.'

Frances had to agree. Part of her mourned for the lost opportunity to be a cherished guest of honour at a flashy party. And yet, proving to British intelligence or whoever Mr Fitzpatrick and Mr Bowman secretly worked for, was by far the most bonzer thing she could imagine. Maybe they would even receive a medal.

'Whoever invented these things deserves a medal.' Tommy welcomed the cool air from the ceiling fan. Apart from a solemn priest, who said a quick prayer in French for the soul of the late Peter Onslow, and two sinewy men in black whom he took for coffin bearers, Aunt Mildred's party were the only people in the funeral parlour. A final farewell, and the body would be sent on its last journey.

Tommy touched his black armband and lowered his head. One felt a bit shabby of course, to be playing at detective at a place like this, but it couldn't be helped.

The rustle of fabric behind him made him turn his neck just enough to see Uncle Sal slip away. Trust the seasoned artist to position himself just right for an unnoticed exit.

Tommy loosened his collar, pretending to be overcome with heat. 'Sorry,' he whispered to his aunt before he followed Uncle Sal.

Outside, he shaded his eyes. He should have taken his

panama hat, only it would have appeared unseemly in a funeral parlour. It took him a full circle before he spied Uncle Sal, 50 yards away half hidden behind an evergreen shrub. Next to him stood another man, with a sallow face. A few more seconds, and the sallow man disappeared from view and Uncle Sal came limping back. Tommy stole back inside the building.

As they filed back out after the coffin had been taken away, Bassington-Whyte whispered to Tommy, 'What was that all about?'

'Bernardo stepped outside for a breather, and I thought, hullo here! He was skulking around behind a bush, with the same fellow as last night. I'm sure of that.'

Aunt Mildred glowered at him, and Tommy fell silent.

Instead of a wake, they had coffee at a small café close to the crematorium and yet far enough to be out of sight. Jack would bring the car around once he had picked up the developed photographs. A taxi would take the ladies home.

'Two more days,' Morris said glumly. 'And then it's stiff upper lip and back to the old treadmill.'

'It's not so bad, is it? Although we will most certainly miss this company and your kind hospitality, Mrs Clifton,' Jordan said.

'Do you think she'll really come to see me?' A lovelorn sigh escaped Morris.

'Our new friend? Absolutely, I mean, she practically promised.' Tommy made a silent note to himself to talk to

Colette about her besotted admirer. That was, unless he happened to be a traitorous murderer.

A limousine came to a halt outside, just before Jack arrived with the Chevrolet. A young man jumped out of the taxi. 'Mesdames?' He flung the door wide open.

'See you at the villa,' Tommy said to his aunt. He signalled for the bill.

'Did you collect the photographs?' he asked Jack, who in return gave him a thick, sealed envelope.

Tommy weighed it in his hands. He rubbed his neck, obviously grappling with a problem.

'What's the matter?' Morris asked.

Tommy slit the envelope open.

'Shouldn't you wait until your aunt is around?' Bassington-Whyte looked to his friends for support.

'What if these really are of the kind she'd rather not have to see? I owe it to her, and we owe it to Onslow that his memory remains unsullied.' Tommy pulled out the first photograph. 'I say, that's strange.'

'What is?' Morris craned his neck. Instead of an answer, Tommy passed the photo to him. It showed a carefully arranged part of a blueprint, together with segments of one of Uncle Sal's letters, which included his name. For the other pictures, Jack had snapped flowers in bloom.

Jordan took the photograph and dismissed it. 'I'd say it was an attempt to see what a new toy can do. At least your aunt won't lose sleep over these pictures.'

'That's true.' Tommy returned the pictures to the envelope.

'Maybe you should destroy the one with the technical drawing,' Morris suggested. 'It might have your aunt thinking otherwise that he was tinkering around with work stuff.'

'Are you sure it's not a frightfully clever new invention, that's worth millions?' A loud chuckle proved that Jordan was only joking.

'I don't think Onslow had the right brain for that. Neither do I, sadly.' Morris shrugged his shoulders.

They entered the house, heading straight up to their rooms to take off the black armbands. On their way to the staircase, Mr Bowman approached them, carrying a silver tray. 'A telegram for you, Mr Bassington-Whyte.'

'Thank you.' The young man snatched the missive. In the background, they could hear a hushed voice speaking on the telephone. 'Half past midnight. Bring the money.'

The young men all looked at each other. Then Tommy chuckled. 'That sounded just like my old roommate at university, when he collected his wins from his bookie. Although usually he was the one who had to cough up.'

'Is that blighter travelling back with us?' Again, Bassington-Whyte's voice held a peevish note. He slapped the unopened telegram in his palm. 'It's bad enough to see my sister and others fawn over him here.'

'No,' Tommy said. 'As far as I'm aware our paths shall part indefinitely. He's on his way to Rome.'

CHAPTER TWENTY-SIX

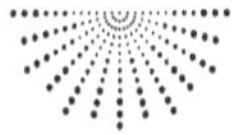

The rest of the day passed in agonising slowness. Aunt Mildred played at cards with the ladies, the men went for a vigorous tennis match, and Frances found herself polishing a brass candle stick over and over, until her fingers hurt.

'That's enough,' Mrs Foster said, 'or you'll wear the metal down.'

Geraldine giggled. 'Not likely, is it?' The maid had bounced back from Mr Bowman's admonitions, but then she didn't seem the sort to dwell on things too much.

'You must be tired.' Mrs Foster took the Brasso tin away from Frances. 'It's been a trying few days for all of us.'

'I was thinking of the poor gentleman, and poor cook. She must have had the fright of her life.' She gave the candle stick one last wipe with a soft cloth.

'Don't. Accidents happen, and it's no good to think back too much.' Mr Bowman entered the butler's pantry in time to overhear Frances's words.

'I swear I've hardly slept a wink since it happened.' Geraldine's mouth turned down at the corners. 'And Mrs Foster as well.'

'Is that true?' Mr Bowman enquired.

'It's only a touch of rheumatism that keeps me awake.' Mrs Foster shot Geraldine a disapproving glance.

'I have a bottle of valerian my former lady used to take. She gave it to me, for railway travel. It might help you,' Frances offered.

'I don't know.'

'But I do, Mrs Foster,' Mr Bowman said. 'We cannot expect you and Geraldine to perform your duties when you're sleep deprived. If you would entrust your pills to me, Frances?'

She curtsied. 'I'll bring them to you right after dinner.'

What she would also bring, was tea laced with a mild sedative. Whatever happened tonight, there were a few people who would enjoy an uninterrupted slumber.

Half an hour after a final cup of tea, while they listened to music on the gramophone, Lady Bassington-Whyte struggled to keep her eyes open. Aunt

Mildred yawned, and Lydia and Anne also declared themselves to be tired.

'I have no idea what's come over me,' Aunt Mildred said, secretly pleased with the effectiveness of the sleeping powder her companions had unwittingly taken with their tea. 'It must be all the worry we have had lately.'

'We all could do with an early night.' Lady Bassington-Whyte signalled the young ladies to follow her. For a moment, she touched her powdered cheek against Aunt Mildred's and smiled. 'I'm quite sure, my dear, that we shall all feel just the ticket in the morning.'

Aunt Mildred squeezed her friend's hand. 'Good night.'

To keep up her pretence, she retired with the other ladies. The gentlemen enjoyed themselves in the games room, judging by their merry voices. She wondered how Uncle Sal coped with what must be an awkward situation, in a company that at best distrusted him, and at worst, harboured sinister plans. Tommy had assured her that all the men had had a chance to study the doctored photograph that clearly connected documents that could potentially be worth a fortune, with Uncle Sal.

In her suite, she poured herself a stiff brandy and bundled herself in her warm dressing gown. Whatever happened, she intended to stay awake.

A triple knock announced Frances. She brought Tinkerbell, after a long and, for the little dog, joyous moonlit walk. 'There is my darling,' Aunt Mildred said. 'Do come in, Frances. He could do with a brush.'

'Yes, ma'am.' Frances grinned, although her nerves were jangling. Jack had warned her not to expect anything to happen before midnight, yet she couldn't help but speculate. Hopefully their quarry was as greedy as he was clever. The prospect of stealing the money Uncle Sal expected should be too much of a temptation to resist.

Only – 'Do you think he'll be in danger?' Frances picked up Tink's favourite brush. As if on cue, he jumped onto her lap and wriggled himself into position for an extended grooming session.

'Sal? I wouldn't worry about that.' Despite her reassuring words, Frances had the creeping feeling that Aunt Mildred shared the same fears. 'I put my trust in Jack, and in Bowman and Tommy.'

'If only we could do something.' Frances smoothed a tiny knot in Tink's fur. The little dog rolled his eyes in sheer bliss.

'We've done ample already, especially you.' Aunt Mildred held up the brandy bottle questioningly.

'A tiny one,' said Frances. The drink would banish the icy feeling in her stomach when she thought about Uncle Sal, having to go out into the night with his bad ankle.

U ncle Sal peered up from a week-old *Times* he had taken from the library. The young men sat around playing penny-ante bridge. 'There should be a piano,' he said. 'We do not have enough music in this house.'

'There's a grand piano in the ball room,' Tommy said, only to receive a vicious kick under the table.

'Don't.' Jordan groaned. 'If we start with one recital, that is the end of our peace.'

'He's right,' Bassington-Whyte agreed. 'First my mother would insist on having a go, and then she would make my sister play and sing for us. I'm sorry, Mr Bernardo, but listening to nothing is better than listening to that.'

'Your sister isn't that bad,' Morris protested.

'You haven't heard her sing in a duet with my mother. They both try to outdo each other. The results are …' He shuddered.

'Like two dogs howling at the moon. I understand.' Uncle Sal chortled. 'It does not matter much, anyway. Tomorrow night I will be on my way.'

'You're leaving a day before us?' Tommy played the last trick of the game, and his bridge partner Morris took over the counting.

Uncle Sal inclined his head. 'Every holiday must come to an end, must it not?'

Tommy stifled a yawn. 'That's a fair point. Speaking of which, what's the final tally?'

'Jordan and Bassington-Whyte owe us two shillings and five pence each.'

'I hate to deprive you of a chance to claw back your colossal losses, but I'm afraid I need to toddle off to get my beauty sleep.' Tommy yawned again.

Uncle Sal closed his newspaper and rose. 'Until breakfast, then.'

'What about one last drink?' Jordan asked.

'Not tonight, thanks,' Tommy said.

'I've had enough as well.' Morris raked in his winnings.

'But it's barely eleven.'

'Sorry, old chap.' Bassington-Whyte clapped Jordan on the shoulder. 'I'm a trifle done in myself.' For once, he had a decided spring in his step as he headed for the door, Tommy noticed. He wondered about the content of the telegram, about which Bassington-Whyte had not mentioned a single word.

As the clock struck midnight, Uncle Sal made his way downstairs. He buttoned up his overcoat and clutched his cane. In the other hand, he held a large white envelope, and his torch.

He had decided against his customary scarf. Although he trusted his ability to fend off an attacker — after all, he had learned enough tricks on and off stage — he also believed in taking as little risk as possible. A scarf offered the opportunity to be grabbed from behind and used to throw him off balance, or worse, strangle him.

He slipped out of the French doors to the garden. An owl hooted and the palm fronds rustled in the light breeze. He forced himself to use the slow, heavy hobble Signor Bernardo was well known for. The hairs on his neck rose as he imagined a silent figure slipping out after him. 'It's only a touch of stage fright,' he told himself, as he fought against the temptation to gaze backwards.

With every step he took, his nerves calmed down. Only 50 yards now, and he'd reach the pine stand where they had searched for the cosh. Keep your head up, he thought. Signor Bernardo, renowned for a certain arrogance, would not look down on his way to an important rendezvous.

His follower kept at a safe distance. The lumbering figure was well ahead now, but he could easily catch up. He fingered the weapon in his pocket. This time, there would be no accident, but then there was no need for that. All it took was a cool head, a little bit of planning, and the will to succeed.

A pebble crunched under his shoe. He froze. No, impossible that anyone could hear him in the dark villa. He crept further down the garden path.

Uncle Sal slowed down even further. Twenty yards, and he would reach the door to the orangerie.

He shone his torch ahead. For one heartbeat, a heavily muffled person stepped out of the deep shadow, only to disappear again. He raised his cane in a greeting. The figure reappeared and stood waiting for him.

'Are you alone?' the man asked as Uncle Sal stopped five steps away from him, so they had the orangerie door between them.

'Of course. Where's my money?'

'Where are my blueprints?'

'Right here.' Uncle Sal held the envelope up high.

The other man produced a fat parcel from his overcoat. 'Always a pleasure doing business with you.'

'Why, what a nice thing to say. Drop the envelopes, please, and stick 'em up, as the say in the pictures. And step closer together.' Gravel crunched as a man with a balaclava over his head pointed his pistol at Uncle Sal's. 'No tricks. I'm a crack shot, if I say so myself.' He took a step forward.

'You can't explain two dead people, even if you could kill us both, and you can't afford to let us get away,' the muffled man said. His voice was barely recognisable as Jack's.

'That depends on you. If you follow my instructions, I will let you walk away. Otherwise, it would pain me to hear that poor Mr Bernardo was accosted by a robber as he took a walk, one assumes for his health, and unfortunately was shot as he valiantly defended himself. Although he did manage to grab hold of the pistol for a moment, just long enough to wound his enemy, who sadly succumbed.' The masked man chuckled merrily. 'But of course, that is entirely up to you.'

'You win.' Uncle Sal waved Jack closer. Jack jumped forward, caught the cane Uncle Sal flung in his direction and dived down as he slammed the cane into their opponent's knee pits. With a pained yelp, the man went down, just as the orangerie door was flung open and hit him.

'Get him, Jack,' Uncle Sal said.

Jack grabbed the masked man's pistol hand and twisted his arm. The weapon fell to the ground, and Jack kicked it away. He held the masked man pinned to the ground. Mr Bowman came out of the orangerie and picked up the pistol. With his other hand, he gave Jack a pair of handcuffs. 'Behind the back, please.'

The masked man grunted. Jack pulled the balaclava off his head and stared into the hate-filled eyes of Dominic Jordan.

'Well done.' Mr Fitzgerald came down the path, accompanied by two burly men. Jordan lay handcuffed and gagged at Uncle Sal's feet.

'We did expect you a little sooner.' Jack brushed the dirt off his knees.

'You appear to have done splendidly without me.'

'He could have shot us.'

'But he didn't.' With a flick of his wrist, Mr Fitzgerald indicated to his companions to take Jordan away. They dragged him to his feet. 'Shall we go up to your room, Sullivan? We don't want to catch a cold.'

'What about the others?' Jack asked.

'Surely they're asleep.'

'I'm pretty sure they're wide awake, and we need their help anyway.'

Mr Fitzgerald gave him a surprised stare.

'Don't you think we should come up with an explanation why Jordan is gone? Which would involve emptying his room and the bathroom of his possessions. Unless you're fine and dandy with the whole affair becoming public knowledge,' Jack said.

Mr Fitzgerald pulled a grimace. 'We should have thought of that, Bowman.'

'I'll take care of it,' the butler said. 'And I'll inform madam of your visit.'

'We could all go to the villa, if we're careful.' Jack wanted to have Uncle Sal inside and in his warm bed as soon as possible. 'My room isn't exactly luxurious.'

'By all means.'

'What about Jordan? Don't you have to go with him?' Uncle Sal inquired.

'Those two men I brought along have enough experience to handle him, until I return to Nice.'

'In that case, what are we waiting for?' Uncle Sal rubbed his cold hands together. 'A spot of whisky wouldn't hurt.'

'Who'd have thought it was Jordan?' Aunt Mildred pursed her lips. 'He seemed so jovial, and well-off too.'

'I didn't suspect him,' Tommy admitted. 'But somebody else did.'

'Who? Why didn't they tell us?' Mr Fitzgerald's face tightened.

'It was Tinkerbell. He never liked him, did you Tink?'

The dog wagged his tail stub and nodded.

Aunt Mildred scooped up her pet and pressed a kiss on his head. 'You're always right when it comes to people.'

Mr Fitzgerald continued. 'We don't know yet, but I have a hunch it will transpire that those convenient payments via Switzerland came from a source other than a deceased relative. He could also have done it for the sport of it. Some people would do anything to prove they're smarter and better than everyone else.'

'Unfortunately, he was smarter than Onslow,' Jack said.

'But not smarter than you.' Frances gave him a rare public kiss.

'You were right about the cipher as well.' Mr Fitzgerald helped himself to a drop of brandy. 'That's why I was late. I received a message from London just before I was heading out.'

'Let me guess,' Jack said. 'Onslow had his eye on our bird, but then Uncle Sal's sudden appearance muddied the waters.'

Mr Fitzgerald nodded. 'Jordan pretended to have found the snapshot of me in Mr Bernardo's possession and hinted at the possibility that I was a dirty dog. That meant,

Onslow wouldn't dream of coming to me, or to anyone in Whitehall, because he had no idea who to trust.'

'Except for Jordan, of course?' Jack probed his knee. He'd hit a rock as he threw himself down, but he'd have a closer look in private, to see if there was real damage.

'He promised he had something else to show Onslow, something he couldn't do inside the villa.'

'He probably made up a cock and bull story about overhearing the planning of a rendezvous,' Jack said. 'The same set-up that worked for us would have fooled Onslow too.'

'That's what the last diary entry hints at.' Mr Fitzgerald eyed his empty glass. 'I'm not going to tell the encryption department a couple of amateurs figured out what these missives said before they broke the cipher. Your guess about dates and certain letters was absolutely correct, Jack, but he had jumbled them up cleverly.'

'It wasn't exactly hard to come to that conclusion.'

Aunt Mildred waved that aside. 'How are you intending to return to your hotel, if your men took your car and that horrible person?'

'I could drive him,' Tommy said. 'Then Mr Fitzgerald can tell me everything that I have missed.'

'I missed most of it as well,' Mr Fitzgerald admitted. 'But I would like to take you up on your offer.' He shook Uncle Sal and Jack's hand. 'Splendid work, gentlemen.'

Jack led the way to the garage. It took him only a few moments to reinstall the distributor cap. 'Let her roll and

I'll push you until you're outside the gate,' he said. 'Then you can start the engine without waking anyone.'

Tommy nodded.

'I'll help push,' said Mr Fitzgerald. 'It's the least I can do.'

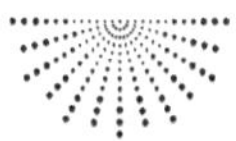

'Where's Jordan? His toothbrush and comb are gone.' Bassington-Whyte held up his coffee cup for a refill. Aunt Mildred gave her butler a quick signal, to be quiet.

'He was called away unexpectedly in the middle of the night,' she said. 'I had Bowman help him pack, so he could reach the first train to Paris.'

'Your butler is commendably quiet, like a cat,' Uncle Sal said. 'I have a very light sleep, and he did not disturb me at all.'

'What a shame about Mr Jordan.' Lady Bassington-Whyte selected a flaky croissant from a basket. 'Just before we all have to leave, too. I hope it is nothing serious. Didn't he have an ailing father?'

'Grandfather, if I remember correctly,' Tommy said.

'It is dashed rotten luck, but we're bound to run into him in the old metropolis.'

'Well, we won't let that spoil our last full day,' Lady Bassington-Whyte said, with an indulgent beam at her children. Her serene mood took Aunt Mildred by surprise.

Bassington-Whyte cleared his throat.

Anne blushed and touched a golden locket around her neck. That must be the infamous piece of jewellery she had originally returned to her beau, Aunt Mildred decided.

'If I could have your attention, I'd like to say something.'

His sister rolled her eyes.

'Miss Deringham has kindly consented to be my wife.' He reached for Anne's hand and showered it with kisses. She gazed at him adoringly.

'You sly fox.' Tommy clapped his hands. 'Not that the lady could have done better. When is the great day to be?'

Aunt Mildred beckoned her butler. 'This calls for a celebration. Bowman, champagne please. You must be so happy for your son, Dorothy. What wonderful news.'

'It's everything I could wish for as a mother.' Lady Bassington-Whyte wiped away a tear of joy. 'Now, if only my darling Lydia were to settle down, I'd be the happiest woman.'

'Mummy, please. You should be grateful that you've found someone wonderful to take Wilfred off your hands.' She winked at Anne.

Mr Bowman brought the champagne.

'A toast,' Tommy said. 'To everyone under this roof.'

'I have a present for the bride,' Uncle Sal said. 'I shall read the cards for all the ladies in this room.' Although this particular trick had been unnecessary to crack Lydia's story about her bracelet, they had decided it would still be useful. Also, Uncle Sal enjoyed it.

Morris gave Tommy an amused chortle.

'We'll take the groom to be off your hands,' Tommy said. 'Is it alright if we borrow Sullivan for a few hours?'

'I'll inform cook that you won't be in for lunch.' Aunt Mildred returned her attention to her guests.

Uncle Sal flung open the French doors and let the mellow sunshine pour into the room. He took his place at a small table the butler had placed so it was sheltered from the breeze, and yet caught the warmness of the air. Two candles sat at both ends. Uncle Sa touched his heart before he lit them.

The ladies sat in a half circle, in an excited mood.

'Who will be the first one to hear what fate has in store for her?' His eyes twinkled as he touched a deck of tarot cards in front of him.

'I'll volunteer,' Aunt Mildred said. To the girls, she whispered, 'It's just a bit of harmless fun.'

'That's what most people say at first.' Uncle Sal wiggled his fingers in the air. 'But my own great-grandmother saved our family from despair and ruin when the cards told her to say no to a Grand Duke when he asked for her daughter's hand in marriage.'

'Why? What had he done?'

'Nothing yet at that stage, but ten years later, he discovered his majordomo had stolen from him, and in a fit of rage, he chased the servant down a hill, and he cut off his head with a sabre. And then he accused his wife of having been hand in glove with the thief, and he locked her into a tower of his castello. She was never seen again.'

Lydia and Anne gasped. Lady Bassington-Whyte' eyes grew wide.

'I'm sure nothing of that sort will threaten to befall me.' Aunt Mildred folded her hands in her lap.

Uncle Sal shuffled the cards before he put the deck down. 'Please cut the deck,' he said. 'Be careful only to use your left hand.'

Aunt Mildred did as asked. He took a quick peek at the bottom card without showing her.

'Now, pose a question. Just one question.'

Aunt Mildred sat still. Her thoughts turned inwards. 'What is the meaning of the last letter my late husband sent me? He said I should search where our hearts met.'

Uncle Sal took two cards from the deck and placed them open on the table. The candle flames flickered.

'The Lovers, and The Fool, both in an upright

position. That is molto bene, very good. Your husband, he was very dear to you.'

She inclined her head.

'The cards say that you have embarked on a new journey, one that is your path alone, but your unity is still there. It is guiding you.' He peered again at the bottom card. 'Where your hearts met. The place where he asked for your hand in marriage. That is where he has put something that you will find, and it will give you strength.'

'But that is …' She frowned. 'The medallion.'

'You understand the message?' Lady Bassington-Whyte clasped her heart. Uncle Sal silenced her with one finger.

'He proposed to me in my mother's drawing room.' Aunt Mildred's voice came from far away. 'We lived there with her, after my father passed away. I still live in the same house. A few months ago, on the anniversary of my dear husband's passing, dear little Tink played with his ball, and it ended up behind a divan. We were unable to reach it, so we had to move the piece of furniture, and next to the ball, there was a golden medallion. Engraved on it were our initials.'

'Take this precious gift along, on all your journeys, and joy will follow.'

Aunt Mildred touched his hand. 'Thank you, Mr Bernardo, from the bottom of my heart.'

'I have a question, too, Mr Bernardo.' Lady

Bassington-Whyte switched places with Aunt Mildred. 'There was a precious thing lost by my husband's ancestor. Where will I find it?'

Aunt Mildred stifled a whoop of joy. They had hoped for just this kind of opening when they had planned the reading for Dorothy's benefit. The cockamamie story they'd made up about her own search for an answer had been a stroke of genius, far-fetched and yet convincing for people yearning to believe.

Uncle Sal shuffled the cards again and made her cut the deck with her left hand. He turned up two cards. 'The Magician, reversed, and Justice, also reversed.' He glanced at the bottom card of the deck. 'I'm afraid, Madam, this man you are talking about, he was not a very respectable man.'

'Maybe not, but times were different,' Lady Bassington-Whyte said with a hint of a pout.

'Davvero, but human nature, it changes not. He was a greedy man, a vain man, and one who did not mind spreading falsehoods to cover up his own failures. The cards, they say, there is no treasure left. There never was such a treasure. It was all a web of lies. The good news is, fortune is still smiling upon you, and upon your family, as we speak.'

'How do you know that?'

'The arcana reveals the truths if we ask the right questions.' He beamed at Lydia and Anne.

'I think maybe I should let my future unfold without finding out too much,' Anne said. 'That is, unless Wilfred is a second Grand Duke who will lock me up in a tower?'

Uncle Sal laughed. 'There is no reason to believe you will be anything but happy.'

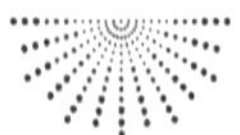

'Tell us everything.' Tommy brought a round of pints from a bar in Nice run by an Englishman who'd married the owner's daughter after his demobilisation. As a shrewd businessman, the bar specialised in being as close to a British pub as possible, including jars of pickled eggs. 'When did you pop the question?'

Bassington-Whyte's face took on a pinkish hue. 'Quite a while ago, actually. Only, not properly.'

'What does that mean? Either you asked the girl to marry you or not.' Morris took a deep swig from his bitter.

'I'd put out my feelers, to see if she'd object to throwing her lot in with me, when lo and behold, the family fortune went down the drain. I couldn't ask a smashing girl like her to marry a pauper, could I?' He sighed. 'And she is smashing, isn't she? She is an angel.'

'They don't come much more charming,' Tommy agreed. 'What changed your mind?'

'I received a telegram form my real estate agent. I'd tried to unload the old family estate, but nobody in their right minds wanted to saddle themselves with a gothic pile, surrounded by farms in the middle of nowhere.'

'I thought you liked the old place,' Morris said.

'I do, but nobody else would. Which is why it was such a stroke of luck that one of the local farmers came up with the lolly to buy the acreage, and the old dairy, leaving me with the house and the park.'

'I'll drink to that.' Tommy raised his glass. 'Cheers.' He checked his watch. 'A spot of lunch before we head back?'

'If Bassington-Whyte pays, now that he's in clover.' Morris chuckled.

'It might stretch to a hot sandwich or two. Pity Jordan isn't here.'

'You can catch up with him another time.' Tommy crossed his fingers behind his back. As far as he was aware, Jordan languished in a prison cell, in solitary confinement. He had no idea what yarn Mr Fitzgerald and the powers-that-be would spin, only that there would be a cover-up story. He wholly agreed. The whole business was bad enough. If Onslow's aunt and sister could be spared the truth, he would do his utmost to play his part.

Thinking of playing parts, he asked, 'What do you really think of Bernardo?'

'I quite like him, even if he is not quite out of the top drawer,' Morris said. 'So what if he really slipped away to meet with someone? We all have a few acquaintances we'd rather not be seen with in public, and yet they're a frightfully good sort. And we shouldn't forget he's a foreigner. They're different.'

'I was wondering if he was pulling our leg.' Tommy drained his glass. 'He would have to be very slow not to notice we were watching him with suspicion.'

'Your aunt said, she didn't trust him,' Bassington-Whyte reminded them.

'That was more my uncle, and who knows, maybe he only didn't trust him with the ladies. That old chap must have been a bit of a heartbreaker in his time.'

'Like Jordan, only more successful?' Bassington-Whyte guffawed. 'I say, is there a jewellery store nearby? I'd like to buy a trinket for my angel.'

Tommy threw down some coins, and they left the bar in high spirits.

'We will miss you.' Aunt Mildred offered Uncle Sal her hand for a final kiss. 'Thank you for your reading.'

'My pleasure.'

Jack held the Chevrolet door open for him.

'Goodbye, everyone. Until we meet again.' Uncle Sal

waved into the round. He spotted Frances watching him from a window upstairs. She must be counting the hours, until she could finally be herself again.

Only one more night, which Uncle Sal would spend again in a hotel in Cannes, and as soon as the Blue Train had pulled out of the railway station, they could enjoy themselves. It was a pity though, that Tommy had to leave as well. Luckily, Aunt Mildred had decided to stay for another fortnight and keep Uncle Sal company. That would give Jack and Frances the freedom to explore.

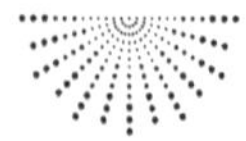

CHAPTER THIRTY

'All alone.' Frances threw herself into Jack arms. She squealed with delight as he twirled her around.

'Don't mind me.' Uncle Sal blinked against the sun.

'You're never in the way.' Jack set Frances down. She kissed her godfather on the cheek. In the background, Mr Bowman discreetly turned his head the other way. Frances wondered how much longer he would stay, until he had tied up the whole affair. Mrs Foster and Geraldine had already left as well, on the normal train, to prepare the London house for Aunt Mildred's return. They would find a telegram at the end of their journey, to inform them that their mistress would be delayed.

Tinkerbell jumped in the air, chasing butterflies again.

Frances closed her eyes in bliss. Two whole weeks,

where Jack could paint and take photographs. They would go for car rides to Antibes and Cannes and into the hills to Cimiez, and feast on picnics where she wouldn't have to lift a single finger. Mr Fitzgerald had presented them with first class tickets on the Blue Train, with an open date. He had also given them a one week stay at a Parisian hotel.

It would be bonzer to have their honeymoon there, Frances thought, yet on the other hand Uncle Sal had looked forward to showing them his Paris for so long.

'You're sighing, kiddo,' Jack said. He lifted her chin up.

'Only because I'm happy, and we have so many wonderful things waiting for us.'

Uncle Sal stole away, towards the house, to give them privacy. In the kitchen, a new cook and a new maid were hard at work, two servants who had no idea that until a few hours ago, Jack and Frances themselves had been the staff. Her maid's uniform was now folded away in her suitcase, as a keepsake.

A lock of hair fell across her forehead.

Jack pushed it back. 'Where shall we go first? The Casino in Monte Carlo? We could get tickets for the opera tonight, and then dine next door, before we walk along the promenade.'

'Lovely.' She refrained from worrying about the costs, just like she had rejected any suggestion of accepting payment for her few days as a maid. She had done a good job though, she thought with a little pride. Geraldine had hugged her farewell and invited her to her wedding. She seemed convinced that Mr Bassington-Whyte would remember her assistance in his betrothal and find employment for her beau.

Frances hoped so too, for Geraldine's sake, and for her own. For it would be impossible to properly visit Aunt Mildred in London, if that would start gossip about her and Jack's undercover work, not to mention Uncle Sal.

Mr Bowman called from the terrace. 'Lunch is ready, Miss Frances.'

Miss Frances! A happy chortle rose in her throat. 'I could get used to that for a bit,' she said to Jack as he took her arm.

'Which part? The one where we're the gentry and others wait on us, or the company?'

'All of it. The sunshine, the food, the heavenly flowers, and the fact that we've caught the villain. At least, you have.'

'A joint enterprise.' Jack's warmth seeped into her skin. 'Like the rest of our lives.'

'But no more dead bodies.' She blew him a kiss and flew upstairs to freshen up before lunch. In a few months, they would be back in Australia, as Mr and Mrs Jack Sullivan. But first, more French adventures awaited, and a delicious lunch.

❧

If you enjoyed this mystery, please consider leaving a review where you bought it or on Goodreads and BookBub. Reviews are important to authors and I want to thank you in advance.

The Jack and Frances mysteries

A Matter of Love and Death

Adelaide, 1931. Telephone switchboard operator Frances' life is difficult as sole provider for her mother and adopted uncle. But it's thrown into turmoil when she overhears a suspicious conversation on the phone, planning a murder.

If a life is at risk, she should tell the police; but that would mean breaking her confidentiality clause and would cost her the job. And practical Frances, not prone to flights of fancy, soon begins to doubt the evidence of her own ears - it was a very bad line, after all.

She decides to put it behind her, but it's not easy. Luckily there is the charming, slightly dangerous night club owner Jack. Jack's no angel - six pm prohibition is in force, and what's a nightclub without champagne? But when Frances' earlier fears resurface, she knows that he's the person to confide in.

Frances and Jack's hunt for the truth puts them in

grave danger, and soon enough Frances will learn that some things are a matter of love and death ...

Murder at the Races

Nothing is a dead-cert against a cold blooded killer …

1931. Frances Palmer is overjoyed when her brother Rob returns to Adelaide as a racecourse veterinarian. But all is not well on the turf, and when a man is murdered, there is only one suspect – Rob.

Frances and her boyfriend, charming night club owner Jack Sullivan, along with ex-vaudevillian Uncle Sal and their friends have only one chance to unmask the real murderer, by infiltrating the racecourse. The odds are against them, but luckily putting on a dazzling show where everything depends on sleight of hand is what they do best.

But with time running out for Rob, the race is on.

Meet Jack Sullivan in *False Play at the Christmas Party*, a novelette set in 1928.

A charity ball in aid of veterans sounded like rich pickings …

Coming soon:

The Case of the Christmas Angel, an Uncle Sal novella

Lights, Camera, Crime!

1932. With his partners-in-crime Jack and Frances off on their honeymoon, retired Vaudeville artist Uncle Sal intends to relive his glory days in London. As a man of many talents, it doesn't take long until his old friend Molly Sweet secures him a small part in one of the new talking picture studios in London.

With his inimitable flair, he soon finds himself at home in front of the cameras, and backstage as well. But there are villains at play whose roles weren't in the script, and Molly and her daughter need Uncle Sal's help. A starring role as a sleuth is nothing new for him, but this time he has to go undercover in a boarding house without the help of Jack and Frances. Can he solve the case of the Christmas angel before his friends' lives are shattered, or will his adventure in the movie world turn into a tragedy?

Meet Alyssa Chalmers, Victorian emigrant, reluctant bride, intrepid sleuth.

The Case of the Missing Bride

Setting sail for matrimony – or something sinister?

1862. When a group of young Australian women set sail for matrimony in Canada, they believe it's the start of a happy new life.

But when one of the intended brides goes missing, only Alyssa Chalmers, the one educated, wealthy woman in the group, is convinced the disappearance is no accident. She sets out to find out what happened.

Has there been a murder?

Alyssa is willing to move heaven and earth to find out the truth. She is about to discover that there is more to her voyage into the unknown than she bargained for, and it may well cost her life …

Inspired by true events.

A Malice Domestic finalist and nominated for a CWA Historical Dagger.

Glittering Death

Gold, wedding bells - and murder!

1862. A group of brides from Australia have arrived in British Columbia, and love is in the air - until the happiness in the prospectors' town "Run's End" is shattered when the hotel-owner is found dead. To make matters worse, something is wrong with the stored gold at the hotel, and an epidemic makes it impossible for anyone to leave town.

The brides pin all their hopes on their friend Alyssa Chalmers to find the murderer and restore peace in their new home. But the killer is cunning, and desperate …

Walking in the Shadow

Quail Island, 1909. Jimmy Kokupe is the miracle man.

On a small, wind-blasted island off the east coast of New Zealand a small colony of lepers is isolated but not abandoned, left to live out their days in relative peace thanks to the charity of the townspeople and the compassion of the local doctor and matron of the hospital.

Jimmy Kokupe is a miracle: he's been cured. But he still carries the stigma, which makes life back on the mainland dangerous and lonely. To find a refuge, he's returned to the camp to care for his friend, fellow patient old Will, and disturbed young Charley.

Healed of his physical ailments and dreaming of the girl he once planned to follow to a new life in Australia, Jimmy meets 'the lady', the island caretaker's beautiful but troubled wife who brings their food. Can she help Jimmy forget his difficult past and overcome his own prejudices towards his mixed parentage, and find the courage to risk living in freedom?

Inspired by true events. Longlisted for the Mslexia award.

Let Sleeping Murder Lie
Love can be the death of you!

American Eve Holdsworth is living her quintessential English dream in a picturesque village in the countryside. Meeting an attractive stranger adds to the appeal.

But Ben Dryden is a pariah in Eve's new neighbourhood, since his wife was murdered five years ago, and he was the only suspect. Eve, who is absolutely sure someone as charming as Ben could never be a killer, is determined to solve the case and clear Ben's name, even if it's against his will.

Soon enough Eve finds herself in deep waters, and with her life at stake, she can only pray that her romantic notions won't be the end of her …

Winner of a Chill With A Book award.

You can catch up with Carmen Radtke on her website (www.carmenradtke.com), on twitter or on Goodreads or follow her on Bookbub.

www.ingramcontent.com/pod-product-compliance
Lightning Source LLC
Chambersburg PA
CBHW050807190726
48285CB00005B/1823